Oct

To: Tommy — a friend
at Concord. Enjoy!

Barbara

GINNY'S DREAM

Barbara Hughes Turner

A novel by
Barbara Hughes Turner

Also by Barbara Turner:

Treasure in Ghost Town

May be ordered through the author at:
63 Meadow Ridge East
Columbia, IL 62236
618-281-6127

ISBN # 1-59457-591-6

Published in the U.S.A. by
Book Surge Publishing
53441 Dorchester Road, Suite 16
N. Charleston, SC 29412

Toll Free: 1-866-308-6235
www.globalbookpublisher.com

Dedication

Dedicated to my family and friends who helped me have a happy childhood such as Ginny had.

Appreciation

I want to thank Stan Nicol for his technical help in preparing my manuscript for publication.

And I want to thank Virginia Austin for taking the picture on the cover, and John Hughes, my brother, for doing the painting for the picture of our old schoolhouse.

I also want to thank Betty Anne Bantz for preparing my manuscript and cover for publication.

Commentary

"The Turner manuscript contributes importantly to understanding family and community life in the rural, poverty-stricken regions of the Midwest in the years 1937–45. But this work is more than an historical novel; It is a revealing portrayal of the joys and anguish—softly understated—of a young girl daring to dream the improbable. Thus, the manuscript could well stand as an informative and inspirational memoir coming from the ranks of the poor and common. . . . Beneath the easy style she evinces, there is a rigor in this work—the characters seemingly real, the cultural facts supportable from our own personal histories in the subject area, the events credible under critical scrutiny."

The late Dr. Robert Hastings
Pastor, Editor of Illinois Baptist Newspaper,
and Reader for Southern Illinois Press at Southern
Illinois University in Carbondale, Illinois

TABLE OF CONTENTS

Chapter 1

The Thorn

It was just a game of tag. I was running as fast as my six-year-old legs would carry me, but when I reached the big old thorn tree that grew at the far west side of our orchard, I stumbled and fell. "Ouch," I yelped. "I sat on a thorn!"

Martha, my older sister, who had been chasing me, ran quickly to my side to see if I was faking or if it was for real. When she saw the tears coursing down my cheeks and the pain registered in my eyes, she didn't ask, but knelt quickly on the ground beside me and put her arms around me. Even at nine years old, it was Martha's nature to comfort those who needed it.

But the pain was too much for me. I needed more comfort than Martha could give. "Take me to Mom," I said in a pitiful voice while the tears continued to flow.

"All right. Just stand up and I'll help you get to the house."

But when I tried to stand the pain was so terrible that I fell against her. "Oh, Martha, I can't walk. It hurts too bad," and the tears flowed faster and faster.

Without another word, my sister lifted me in her arms and carried me across the orchard which our parents had planted when they were first married, across the shady side yard, and around to the back porch. By this time, I was screaming, partly from pain and partly from knowing I would soon get help and relief.

As she laid me down on the back porch, my mother came running from the kitchen with Janice close behind her. Janice was my little sister who was just two last week and she followed our mother everywhere. Rover, our big brindled watch dog, disturbed by the commotion, began to bark, and even Bobby Dog, our little rat terrier, roused from his nap, moved from one sunny spot to another.

"What in the world is the matter?" my mother asked for the sight of her made me cry louder and harder. She knelt on the rough boards of the porch and took me in her arms. She wore a faded housedress and apron, and her feet were bare as they usually were all summer, there was a smudge of flour on her face from her baking, and her dark red hair was pulled tightly back in a bun at the back of her head which made her look much older than her thirty-five years, but to me she looked like a guardian angel, and I clung to her fiercely.

"I . . . I fe . . . . " I tried to talk, but I was crying too hard.

"We were playing tag, and she stumbled and fell," explained Martha. "She said she sat on a thorn and it did happen under the old thorn tree, but when I tried to help her up to walk to the house, she cried harder and said that she couldn't stand or walk, so I carried her."

Mom wiped my tears on her apron and cuddled me close in her arms. Although there were six of us children, her love was always enough for each of us. "Let's take a look," she said practically. And so saying, she stretched me out on the porch, slid off the porch to the ground and pulled up my short cotton dress, and down my panties so she could see my small behind. "Well, there's nothing here but a red spot," she said, but when she touched the red spot, I yelled in pain.

"Maybe the thorn went inside," said practical Martha as she edged close to take a look while Janice rubbed my head and said in her tiny chirpy voice, "Ginny, Ginny."

"Maybe it did," Mom agreed. "Sit here with her, Martha, while I go get a piece of fat meat and a clean white rag. We'll put a bandage on it holding the fat meat against the spot and maybe it'll work the thorn out. That's what my grandma always did when I stepped on something and stuck it in my foot."

We all knew that Mom had lived with her grandma after her own mother died when she was a little girl so we were used to being treated by her remedies. Living in Southern Illinois in the thirties as we did, homemade cures were always used.

Mom went back in the kitchen while I lay sprawled on the back porch face down with Martha beside me holding my hand while Janice patted my head and Rover kept trying to lick my face. Martha pulled down my dress and kept saying, "It'll be all right. It's be all right." She was probably feeling guilty because she had been chasing me.

After Mom had put the fat meat on the red spot, covered it with the white rag, and tied it into place with strips of cloth around my leg, she gathered me up into her own capable arms and carried me around the house, up on the front porch and into the bedroom where she turned back the quilt and deposited me in bed, dirty feet and all.

"You stay there and rest this afternoon," she said as she washed my face with a wet washrag and smoothed back my heavy dark curls. "The fat meat will draw out the thorn and by morning you'll be as good as new."

I wanted to argue that it was a beautiful sunshiny afternoon in late June, and I'd really rather be outside playing, but it did hurt very much if I moved about much so I decided to just lie still and rest.

"I'll send Elizabeth to read to you when she gets back from Miss Whitfield's. She went to borrow some baking powder so I could fix some cornbread for supper." She left and I closed my eyes.

I must have gone to sleep for the next thing I heard was Elizabeth's cheerful voice, and opening my eyes I saw her coming over to the bed. Elizabeth was thirteen, a thin girl with short cropped blonde hair and blue eyes. She seemed to live in a dream world, and was always hiding away in the hayloft, or back at the bluff, and was always writing poetry. But she was gentle and kind and I loved her dearly.

"Ginny, whatever did you do to yourself?" she asked as she leaned over to give me a kiss. Martha said you sat on a thorn. Is that true?"

I gave her a pitiful nod as the tears welled up in my eyes again. She kissed me again and sat down on the bed beside me. "Mom said for me to read to you, and I have some of my poems hot off the press."

She read me her poems and as always I told her they were beautiful. I wanted to get up, but when I even sat up, it hurt too badly and I sank back down on the pillows. When Mom called Elizabeth to come help her, I just lay there listening to the sounds from the kitchen and outside.

When Daddy and Joey came in from the fields, they came in to see me. Joey, my older brother was fifteen, and had coal black hair and dark eyes and freckles across his nose just like I did. He just said that he was sorry I was hurt, looked at me awkwardly awhile then left to do the chores. But Daddy pulled up a chair to the bedside, took my hand in his and smiled down at me. I loved Daddy so much, and I knew he had a special love for me. Elizabeth said it was because I was born right after his beloved daughter Alice by his first wife had died of pneumonia, and I had helped take her place.

Daddy had been real sick and had been in the hospital for two years, or so Martha said, as it just seemed like such a long time to me. I liked when it was my turn to go with Mom in the car with one of the uncles, or Grandpa on the long trip to see him, but I did not like him being away. He had only come home this spring. He seemed all right, but I had heard Joey tell Mom one night when I was supposed to be asleep that they would have to go on running the farm as they had done all the time he was gone, and it seemed that they were doing just that. Daddy just seemed quiet and peaceful, and glad to be home.

Now, I squeezed his hand as I looked up at him through my tear filled eyes, and said, "I fell and hurt myself real bad, Daddy, but Mom put fat meat on it and she says I'll be good as new by morning."

"I'm sure you will be, Punkin," he said as he held my hand tighter. He usually called me Punkin even though he knew my name was Ginny. He had wanted to name me Rhody for his little sister who had fallen in the fireplace and died from her burns, but Mom had insisted that I be called Ginny after a character in one of her favorite books. I had always been glad that she had won, but I never told him that.

We stayed like that for a long time until Mom stuck her head around the door and said in her kindly though reproving voice, "Joe, don't you think you had better go help Joey and Elizabeth with the chores?" Then he smiled and nodded and got up and left.

I liked being served supper in bed, and the attention they gave me with one and then another coming to sit with me to talk, read to me, or just sit by my bed, but I didn't like being isolated there while all the fun and excitement of our large family took place in the other rooms, or on the long front porch.

When it got dark, Mom came with a lighted kerosene lamp and a washpan of warm water to wash my feet and get me into my nightgown. When she had me sit up on the side of the bed and stick my feet down in the water, I cried out in pain for the place on my backside hurt so much. After I was ready for bed, she sat on the side of the bed beside me and stroked my forehead.

"I'm sure the fat meat will work and you'll feel better in the morning," she said. It was the year 1937, and this was the best way she knew to draw out splinters and thorns if they were so enbedded that she couldn't pick them out with a needle.

"Now, let's say your prayers so you can get to sleep." She had given me an aspirin for the pain , and I was feeling sleepy.

"Do I have to kneel by the bed?" I asked. "It hurts when I move about."

"No, just close your eyes and fold your hands, and I'm sure God will hear your prayers."

So, I prayed. "Dear God, bless Mom and Daddy, and Naomi, Joey, Elizabeth, Martha, Janice, Rover, and Bobby Dog, and all our friends. Amem." I opened my eyes then closed then quickly. "And please God, help me to get well."

She kissed me, took the lamp and left the room. I must have fallen asleep soon afterwards. It was much later for it was very dark and still when I awoke feeling like I was burning up. I was thrashing about and crying, and I heard Martha spring up from where she slept beside me, and run to call Mom.

Mom came with the lamp, but when she had felt my forehead and saw the state I was in she sent Martha to get Daddy. I remember him coming in the room pulling up his overalls as he came. He took me up in his arms and sat down in the rocker. I can still hear him saying, "She's burning up with fever. Go get a pan of cold water and some towels." While Mom ran to do his bidding, he laid me back on the bed and had Martha help pull off my nightgown. Then while I lay there in my panties feeling as though my body were on fire, he began to bathe me with the cold wet towels. Sometime after that I slept. I didn't know until much later that one or the other of my parents stayed by my bedside all night, feeling my head, and bathing my body when I felt too hot.

Next morning, I was not as good as new and the fat meat had not drawn out the thorn or whatever it was. Instead, when they took off the bandage, the small red spot was now a huge red place with streaks of red running out in all directions which was a sure sign of blood poisoning. I saw the fear in my mother's eyes as she looked down at it, and saw her lips moving in a silent prayer.

It was Daddy who said, "We've got to get her to a doctor." And turning to Joey who stood with my sisters around the foot of the bed, he said, "Joey, run up to Uncle Albert's and see if he can take us." As Joey left at a run, I knew that Daddy was again in control.

Uncle Albert drove Joey back, and before I quite knew what had happened, they had my clothes on me and we were away in the car leaving Elizabeth and Martha to take care of Janice.

When we got to the doctor's office, Daddy lifted me up in his arms and carried me inside. Uncle Albert had called before he came for me and they were waiting. Daddy carried me right into the examining room and laid me down on the long steel table. The doctor came in wearing his white coat. He was old and looked mean and I felt scared, but his voice was kind and his hands were gentle as he turned me over on my stomach and lifted my dress.

"Well, what have we here?" he asked as he looked at my red behind with the streaks running out from it. Then he touched the spot and I jumped and screamed out in pain. "What did you do?" he asked.

"I fell down on a thorn," I said with a sob in my voice. "Martha and I were playing tag and she was chasing me, and I fell, but it wasn't Martha's fault."

"I'm sure it wasn't," said the doctor. "I don't mean to hurt you, but I've got to feel this to see if the thorn is still in there. Try to be real brave." As he began to feel and probe, I gritted my teeth and tried to be a big girl.

"The fat meat didn't work," I said while I tried hard not to cry.

"Fat meat?" he questioned.

"Yes," my mother answered. "I always use fat meat when they step on thorns or splinters, and it nearly always draws them out, but this time it didn't do any good."

"Yes, I've heard that does often work," the doctor said. I guess he knew that because of the Depression in which we lived that many people tried home remedies instead of going to the doctor.

He continued to feel and press and touch, and sometimes I cried out in pain, sometimes I was very brave.

My parents stood one on each side of me holding my hands and giving me support.

Finally, he put a dressing on it, and helped me lay over on my side. Calling my parents over to the far side of the room, he talked in a low voice, but I could hear what he said. "I don't think the thorn is still in there, but I don't understand the inflammation and the fever. I put some salve on it which should draw out anything in there, and I'll give you some to put on several times a day. I'll also give you some medicine for the infection and the fever. But if she isn't better, I'd better see her in about two days.

In the meantime, keep her quiet and in bed."

The day after my trip to the doctor, Naomi came home for the weekend as she always did. Even though she was only sixteen, she worked a full time job doing all the cooking, cleaning, and laundry for a neighboring family where the mother had been very ill since the birth of her last child. They had four little boys so there was a lot of hard work for Naomi, but she had helped Mom since she was knee high to a grasshopper, a favorite expression of Daddy's, and she was a good worker and a cheerful person. She hadn't been able to go to high school because Mom couldn't afford to pay the bus and book fees so she had either helped Mom, or hired out since she was through eighth grade.

Naomi was my oldest sister and she was my favorite. The reason probably being because she had always spoiled and made over me, and often brought me gifts especially if she had had a chance to go to town. Now, I felt happiness sweep over me as I heard her voice in the next room. I could hear all of them telling her about me being sick, taking me to the doctor, and what he had done. I felt jealous that they were taking her time when I needed her with me so I called out in my most pitiful voice.

"Naomi, Naomi, come see me."

Almost immediately she came through the door and over to my bed. Leaning over, she gave me a hug and a kiss. As always, she smelled good, and I loved her hugs.

"Well, Ginny," she said as she laid me back against the pillows and sat down on the side of the bed. "I hear that you got hurt and had to go to the doctor." That in itself was really something in those days.

I felt the tears well up in my eyes as I looked up into her gentle brown ones. Sympathy and love has always reduced me to tears in times of stress. For a long time, she sat by me holding my hand and telling me about her week. Finally, she felt that she had to go help Mom for even though she was home such short periods of time, she always felt obliged to help.

Each week when she came home while I was in bed she brought me a gift, even if it were just a ripe peach, or a piece of cake she had made for the family. But one week, she brought me a special gift, the most special gift I ever had as a small child. I was looking out the window when she got out of Mr. Marvin's car, and I saw that she was holding a big long box. She came straight to my bedroom with the others trailing along behind her.

"I've brought you a very special gift, Ginny," she said. She placed the box on the foot of my bed and opened it. Then she handed to me the most beautiful doll I had ever seen. It had long blonde hair and painted blue eyes, and was dressed in a pink organdy dress and even had on panties and shoes and socks. I was so happy that I cried as I hugged it to me.

I found out a long time later that Mrs. Marvin had given it to her to bring to me. It had belonged to their little girl who had died of typhoid fever. Mrs. Marvin had given up hopes of ever having another little girl so had decided to give it to me. It wouldn't have mattered even if I had known then for it became my constant companion in bed, and the most precious thing I ever had.

My other sisters were good to sit with me, either talking, or playing games, or sometimes they read to me. Even little Janice would come and crawl up on my bed, pat me on the head, and say, "Poor Ginny," like I were a pet. Joey came in every day to see how I was feeling, and once he brought me some little animals that he had whittled out of wood. I loved them and played with them often. Daddy spent long hours in the evenings sitting by my bedside, telling me stories, or singing to me, and even Mom in her busy busy schedule found time for me each day. Often in the middle of the night, I woke up to find Mom kneeling by my bed praying for me to get well. Even in my small child's mind, I knew my mother had great faith in God.

My favorite thing to do as a child was to play paperdolls that we cut out of catalogs, making the furniture out of paper, and bending the dolls so they could sit. The person I most enjoyed playing this with was Ellen, a friend of ours who was Martha's age, but who spent long hours playing with me. She came often to see me while I was sick, and if I felt well enough, we played paperdolls, covering my bed with the furniture and paperdolls. Martha usually played for awhile then she went off to watch Janice, help Mom, or do something on her own. Martha, like Naomi, was always Mom's faithful helper.

It ended up that I spent six long weeks in bed, taking medicine, putting salve on the sore place, and going to the doctor two or three times a week. Since we didn't have a car, getting to the doctor was always a problem, and now it was a major one. The older ones so hated asking relatives, or neighbors to take me that it was usually Martha who got this unwanted task. I knew because I had often heard Joey or Elizabeth's voice raised in protest. But when it became such a long drawn out thing, people volunteered to drive on certain days, and soon a schedule was worked out. I know that my parents were deeply grateful to these dear people. Mom always went with me, holding my head on her lap in the back seat. Sometimes, Daddy went if it were rainy and he couldn't work in the fields. I was always glad when he went.

It soon became evident that the doctor was very puzzled with my case. Sometimes the red lines would go away and at other times they were back. There would be no fever for days; then I would wake up in the middle of the night burning up. The huge red place on my bottom stayed, and the pain became more intense. I cried out in pain when they stood me on my feet, or even dangled my legs over the side of the bed. I was weak from staying in bed so long, and I lost weight. I was often cross and fretful. Twice the doctor lanced the place, which meant he cut into it with a sharp pointed knife while they held me down, and I screamed in pain.

Finally, at the end of the six weeks, he decided that he must put me to sleep and dig deeper to see if the thorn were still in there. While I lay on his table, he explained to me what he was going to do. My mother, father, and Ellen's father who had driven us were all in the room too. He put a mask like thing over my face filled with ether to put me to sleep. After a little bit, I could hear him say to my parents, "I wonder if she's asleep."

I can remember answering in a groggy voice, "Yes, I'm asleep," and they all laughed.

He waited until I was really asleep then he cut deep into my bottom, and they said that the pus and corruption coming out of it flew across the room striking Ellen's father in the chest. And there laying in the mess on the table was the thorn, really a rather big one that had lain embedded inside me all those weeks. As I look back on this now, I realize that today there would have been a big malpractice suit, with my parents probably getting a lot of money, but then there were only my mother's prayers of thanksgiving that it was over, and I was going to be all right.

Chapter 2

The Watermelon

It was the next summer when Ellen and I stole the watermelon. We hadn't stolen anything before, and we haven't stolen anything since, but on that hot July afternoon the temptation was too great and we yielded.

Ellen had come up to our house to play paperdolls, but it was stifling hot in the bedroom with the windows closed, and if we opened them, the paperdolls and their furniture blew all over the place. So, after a few minutes we decided to go down to the creek and go wading. We asked Martha to go with us, but she was busy rocking the new baby that had been born in May. Her always feeling that she had to be helping was downright depressing to Ellen and me both. So, we told her to tell Mom where we were going, and took off for the creek.

By the time we got there, we were hot and sweaty so the cold water felt wonderful to our hot dusty feet. We even knelt down on the rocks and splashed some water up on our flushed faces. Then we sat on the huge rocks, dangled our feet in the water, and talked. Ellen and I always loved to talk to each other.

Suddenly there was a noise in the bushes, and looking up quickly we saw our two milk cows, Susie and Old Jersey with her new baby calf staring down at us as though we were the intruders. After looking at us for a few minutes while they solemnly chewed their cuds, they came down the bank and into the water where they drank some, and then just stood there enjoying the coolness of the water.

After awhile Ellen said, "Wouldn't a nice big watermelon taste good right now?"

I smacked my lips at the thought of it. "Yes, it really would," I agreed.

"Did your daddy raise any this summer?" she asked.

"No," I answered. "Did yours?"

She shook her close cropped blonde head. "No, after that big crop of strawberries, he didn't want to fool with watermelons."

I remembered the strawberries because Martha and I had gone down and picked some to earn some pocket money. It had been hard backbreaking work, but we felt proud of the money we had earned.

"Old Mervin has some," I said. "He has a whole great big patch. I saw them when I went with Daddy last week to take the sorghum to his mill."

"Yes, he does. My daddy bought one from him a few days ago," she agreed.

We sat for a long time in silence and I thought about Old Mervin. He was a very old man, or so I thought, with white hair and a long flowing bristly moustache. Most of us kids were afraid of him for he seemed cross and mean. I had heard people say that he had read the Bible over and over and knew it better than any preacher so he could argue with the evangelists who visited him every summer during our revival to try to convert him. But he never came to church, and he was never converted, so he was sure going to Hell when he died. I guess I thought of him as the Devil.

He lived in a little ramshackle house just across the bridge from our creek where we were now sitting. He lived alone now with his old hound dog since his wife had died. She had been sick a long time and Mom used to send her food and stuff, especially at Christmas time. I remembered going once with Elizabeth and Martha, and I thought she looked like a skeleton laying there on her old featherbed. He farmed a small plot of ground, and also had a mill to grind sorghum into molasses, the thick sweet syrup that Daddy loved on his hot biscuits. But most of all, he was known for the big watermelon patch that he raised each summer. It was that watermelon patch that I was thinking about just now.

To this day, neither of us will admit that we suggested it, but after looking at each other for awhile, it seemed to be mutual consent, we were on our feet running along the bank for the bridge. We climbed over the banisters and down into his side of the creek.

"We'll have to be very quiet in case he's around," whispered Ellen, "So we better not walk in the water."

I agreed with a nod of my head, and we cautiously crept along in the gravel with our hardened bare feet. I think part of the excitement of it was that we might be caught.

After going a few yards in this way, we felt that we were near enough to the watermelon patch to risk a look. So, we carefully climbed up the bank and peered around in all directions. We could see his house with his dog asleep on the porch, but he was nowhere in sight though we looked in all directions. And there right in front of us was that wonderful watermelon patch with "thousands" of melons just laying there waiting to be picked. We scrambled up the bank and began to walk up and down the rows.

"Which one shall we take?" asked Ellen still talking in a whisper.

"Might as well be a big one," I whispered back.

"I guess so," she giggled nervously. "Might as well get all we can while we're doing it."

"How about this one?" I pointed to a huge green striped melon lying at my feet.

"Looks good," she whispered. "But how can we tell if it's ripe?"

"Daddy always thumps them," I remembered. So we knelt there in the dirt and thumped the big melon with our small inexperienced fingers, but we could not tell.

Then forgetting our caution, and need to be quick and quiet, we walked up and down the rows, thumping the melons, trying to find a ripe one. But suddenly, on hearing the rattle of a team and wagon coming down the road, we grabbed the nearest one, and dashed down the bank into the creekbed, and literally ran for the bridge where we hid underneath it while the wagon rumbled overhead. Imagine our surprise and dismay when we peeked out and realized that it was Old Mervin turning in at his barnyard! We were saved being caught by just seconds!

Since Ellen was older and bigger than me, she carried the melon as we scurried back to our side of the creek. Then climbing up the bank, we ran as fast and as far as we could. Finally, exhausted we sank down on the grass under an old willow tree that hung out over the creek laying the melon between us. Then realization struck us both at the same time. We had no knife to cut the watermelon with, and nothing to eat it with! And we certainly couldn't take it home with us.

"How will we cut it?" I asked, and suddenly the whole idea did not seem like such a good one after all.

"I don't know," Ellen replied, and because the same idea had come to her she sighed and said, "I guess we shouldn't have taken it." Then she took my hands in hers and staring into my green eyes with her blue ones, she solemnly said, "Ginny, we mustn't ever tell anyone about this, or we'll be in big trouble. Understand?"

Slowly I nodded my dark curls. "I know, Ellen, let's do that pledge that the big kids do. You know, the one about

'I promise never to tell, and if I do I hope to die.' Think that will work?"

She thought about it awhile then nodded her head so we held hands and said the pledge together even though I didn't much like the part about dying. I didn't hope to die now, or ever. But it did make us feel better, and we went back to the problem of how to cut the melon.

"I know!" I shouted. "Let's throw it on the ground and bust it. Then we can eat the pieces."

"Good idea," agreed Elled, and picking up the melon, she stood up and threw it with all her strength, and it fell to the ground with force breaking open and falling apart in several pieces.

We stood just staring unable to believe for the melon was not mouth watering red and delicious looking, it was not even pink, but was "green as a gourd" as Daddy always said about something that was not ripe. The melon we had stolen was not even fit to eat!

"Do you suppose that's God's punishment for us being wicked?" I asked in a whisper as though I were still afraid of being overheard.

But Ellen in her ten year old wisdom shook her head. "I don't think so. I think it's just bad luck."

"Well, what are we going to do with it? We can't just leave it lying there for Elizabeth to see when she roams up and down the creek making up poetry, or for Daddy to find when he comes down to plow the corn. What are we going to do?"

"I know," said Ellen, and she picked up a stick and began to dig a hole in the sandy soil.

"Good idea." I snatched up a stick and began to help her. "We'll bury this old green melon, and no one will ever know about it."

"Except us."

"Yeah, except us," and suddenly I had this terrible feeling in the pit of my stomach as I realized this terrible thing we had done.

It took a long time to dig a hole big enough for all the pieces, but we finally finished, pushed them into the hole, and covered them over with the dirt. Then we walked back and forth across the hole with our bare feet until it was packed firmly in place.

For days I worried that the watermelon seeds, even though the watermelon was green, might begin to grow, push through the dirt, and a big watermelon vine would begin to grow there that would have to be explained. I knew things like that could happen for just that spring when I had been sent to help Martha plant beans next to each stalk of corn, I had grown weary of the task long before we were through, and I had dumped a whole handful of beans instead of the two I was supposed to plant in one hole and covered them over. When there was a riot of bean sprouts in one spot, I had some explaining to do. Now, would I have a watermelon vine to explain too?

When we had finished burying the green melon which was the evidence of our crime, we went back down in the creek to wash our face and hands and our dirty feet. Then we decided to go home so up the road we went. When we reached our orchard which was now minus the old thorn tree for Daddy and Joey had cut it down and burned the wood after my accident last summer, Ellen decided that she had best get on home so we said good-by.

But she had only gone a few yards when she turned and called to me, "Ginny," and when I answered she held her finger up to her lips and then crossed her arms over her heart as a reminder of our pledge not to tell. I nodded and waved then slowly dragged myself up the lane to the old farmhouse.

I heard laughter and talking from the back porch so wandered around the house to see what was up. My whole family was there, even Naomi who was now working for our uncle Tobias who lived in Carmon, the town about seven miles away. He had gone down to see his daughter Vivian who lived on the farm down past ours, and Naomi had come along for a visit. Daddy was sitting on the edge of the porch holding in one hand a huge green striped watermelon and in the other a big butcher knife. While I stood there and stared open mouthed, he thrust the knife into the melon and split it open. It was not green and icky looking like the one we had just stolen and buried, but it was red ripe and delicious looking. My brother and sisters were gathered around him eagerly awaiting the slice that he handed them as he cut them one by one. Then they moved over to the grass where they leaned over to keep from dripping it on them, and enjoyed the delicious fruit.

It was Mom, who was sitting in an old wooden rocking chair nursing the baby, who looked up and saw me standing in the background staring at them.

"Why, Ginny," she called in her loving voice. "I'm glad you're home. Come and have some watermelon."

Then they all turned and looked at me, and Naomi said, "Hi, Ginny, how's my girl?"

Usually I would have run to run to hug her, but not today. I just stood there too upset to move fearing that I knew where that watermelon had come from.

"Come have some melon, Punkin," said Daddy holding out the last piece. "Old Mervin just brought it a little while ago, and we decided to try some while Naomi was here to enjoy it."

But when I shook my head, he offered it to my mother. She too declined saying, "I'll have some when I finish feeding Alice."

"Then I guess I'll try it," said Daddy as he bit into the luscious looking red melon. "Say, Old Mervin has outdone himself. That's really delicious."

"I'll say," agreed Joey. "Cut another one." He threw his rind in the old dishpan used for pigs' slop and came back to the porch.

"Another one? He had brought more than one," I thought to myself as the tight place in my stomach got tighter and tighter.

"Get another one out," said Daddy, "And I'll cut it up. We won't need any supper, Pauline," he said to my mother, "If we keep on eating these."

"Look under the house, Ginny," cried Elizabeth who had joined Joey for another piece. "Old Mervin brought a whole wagon loan and we put them under the house to keep them cool."

I leaned over to look thinking that at any minute I would throw up while Joey crawled under the house and pulled out another big melon. There were "tons" of melons under there, melons that Old Mervin had brought up here and given my family while Ellen and I had been stealing one miserable green melon from his patch. Now, I was really sick.

The girls who had finished their pieces and were coming back for more called out to me how good it was, that I must try some, and what in the world was wrong with me anyhow? Little Janice, her face all smeary with watermelon juice, came over and put her sticky hand in mine. "Try some, Ginny. It's good." Her short blonde hair bounced up and down in delight, and her blue eyes twinkled. I wiped my hand on my dress and made my way to the porch.

Daddy had cut open another red ripe melon, and they were all reaching for their pieces. I went up on the steps and started for the back door, but Mom's voice stopped me. "Ginny, are you sick? I've never seen you turn down watermelon. You've always loved it."

"No, I just don't want any," I said and moved on toward the door and safety.

But Mom said, "Come here and let me feel your head," which was always her way to determine if we had fever. I went over to her and she felt of my head, but as

I knew it would be it was cool to her touch. It was my heart and stomach that were killing me, and I couldn't tell her that. "Are you sure you don't want any?"

"I'm sure."

"Did Ellen go home?"

I nodded my head. Then I said, "My stomach kinda hurts. I'd like to go lie down awhile."

She smiled then looked down at the now sleeping baby in her lap. "How about taking Alice with you? Looks like she's already asleep." She took the baby from her breast, buttoned up her dress, and handed her up to my waiting arms. As I escaped to the kitchen, I heard her call out to my father, "Ok, Joe, cut me a big piece of watermelon."

That night I had trouble sleeping, and in my nightmare Old Mervin was chasing me, then he had a pitchfork, and then he was the Devil. I woke up frightened and panicked. I wanted dreadfully to tell Mom, but I had promised Ellen, and I believed that I should keep that promise so I did.

When Sunday morning came, I decided that I didn't feel like going to Sunday School, but after Mom felt my head to see if I had fever, she decided that I would go. So I set off with my older sisters and brother dressed in my best clothes to walk the three miles to the little Baptist church where we went every Sunday unless it was pouring rain, or we were having a blizzard. Mom seldom got to go, but she always sent us.

And wouldn't you know that just like he knew, the old minister who preached once a month at our church, preached that Sunday morning on the Ten Commandments with the Eighth One screaming out at me, "THOU SHALL NOT STEAL." I dared not look at Ellen either during the sermon or afterwards.

And when they cut another watermelon that night, I still couldn't eat any. They all questioned me, unable to understand why anyone could pass up such a tempting food. I felt miserable and I still couldn't sleep well.

Ellen came up the next morning to play, and when Martha showed her the melons under the house and told her about Old Mervin bringing a wagonful, she flashed me an astonished look. I nearly died.

For almost a week I suffered my sin in silence, wanting to tell Mom, but remembering my oath to Ellen, refusing to eat the luscious looking melons that my family enjoyed every day, but feeling that it would never go down my constricted throat. Finally, I could stand it no longer. I went to Mom one afternoon when she sat in the living room feeding the baby. I stood in front of her, first on one foot and then the other. Then she asked in her understanding voice as she always did.

"Ginny, what on earth is the matter with you? You've been acting strange all week. Come on, tell me what's wrong." She held out her free arm, and I went into the circle of it.

"Oh, Mom," I blurted out. "I've done a terrible sin, and I'm probably going to go to Hell."

Her expression changed to one of pure concern. "Ginny, what did you do? Nothing could be that bad. Now, tell me and you'll feel better."

Then while tears coursed down my cheeks I told my story through my sobs. "Well, Ellen and I were playing down at the creek the other day, and we got hungry for watermelon, and we knew that Old Mervin had oodles of them so we crawled under the bridge, sneaked up to his patch, and, Mom, we stole one of his melons, and carried it back to our side of the creek. But then we didn't have any knife to cut it and we had to smash it on the ground. And, Mom," now my sobs got louder. "It was green as a gourd and we couldn't even eat it. So, we buried the pieces in the sand like I did the beans that day, and we came home and there you all were eating watermelon, and Old Mervin had brought the whole load, and I just couldn't eat any, and I can't stand it anymore, and the preacher preached about breaking the Ten Commandments and, and—"

"Oh, Ginny, Ginny," I couldn't tell if my mother were laughing, or crying, but she drew me close to her in a giant hug. "What you did was very wrong, but you're not going to Hell because of it. You can ask God to forgive you and He will. I really should make you go ask Old Mervin to forgive you," but seeing the look of distress in my eyes, she added, "But I won't. Kneel down here and ask God to forgive you now."

I did and I felt so much better. The terrible hot feeling in the pit of my stomach was suddenly gone, but it was a long time before I could enjoy, truly enjoy watermelons again. And when I finally confided in Ellen that I had repented and told my mom, she just laughed and said,

"Oh, yeah, I told my mom that very night," I felt like committing the sixth Commandment.

Chapter 3

Stolen Lunch

That fall I was in the third grade at the little country school where Martha and I attended. I had had my eighth birthday in August so I felt much older. Since Rex, who had been in the second grade with me, had failed, I was in third grade all by myself as I would be in fourth, fifth, and sixth grades. Years later I would brag that I had been the smartest one in my class, and if they didn't know what kind of school I had gone to, I wouldn't have to add that I was also the dumbest. Martha and Ellen were in sixth grade with the three boys that they went all the way from first to eighth grades with, but I was always alone.

Along with Ellen, my other best friend was another Ginny who was in fourth grade along with Bill Matthews who lived about two miles on down our mailbox road. Ginny was Rex's older sister and we were friends for many years. Her father had been killed in a wheat threshing accident when she was quite small. There were ten children in her family with her and Rex being the youngest. They lived on a big farm about three miles directly south of us. I loved to go to their house as it was much nicer than ours, and I liked to pretend that it was my house. But I would never have traded my mother for hers.

In our school, there were usually about thirty students with one teacher. The teacher was a man, who farmed in the spring and summer, and taught us in the fall and winter. Looking back, I realize that they didn't know much about teaching, but I guess we learned by hearing things repeated over and over and over. My first and second grade teacher always wore a black suit, never smiled, and sat on the piano stool to hear our lessons. I stood beside him once each morning reciting my primer for I was not taught phonics. I doubt if he even knew what phonics was. I could repeat from memory:

Peter was a boy. Peggy was a girl.
Peter had a dog. Peggy had a cat.

But my teacher in third grade, Mr. Grafton, was a fun person who was always laughing and telling jokes, and if we begged him real hard, he'd stand on his head on top of his desk and sing to us, "When Rattlesnakes Lay Eggs". He didn't do that much after the County Superintendent came to visit one day and caught him in the act. And he was more careful how he answered a knock at the door after he called out, "Come in if your nose is clean," and the County Nurse walked in with a frown on her face.

But he was lots of fun, and he often played games with us at recess, morning and afternoon, and sometimes even the long one after we ate our lunches. My favorite was always "Stink Base" where if you got caught, you had to stay on their base until you were rescued. You stood with your arm outstretched hoping someone would get through the lines to rescue you. In the fall, he usually spent the long recess practicing basketball on our outdoor court with the older boys since they got to play in the county tournaments in Carmen in February. And in the spring, he spent long hours, even taking school time, to practice with all the older boys and girls for the county track meet which was also held in Carmen in late April. We swang, or played our own games while they ran races up and down the dirt lane that led east towards our house, or practiced high jumping, pole vaulting, or throwing the shot put.

One such spring day in early April Ginny and I sat in the warm sun on the school porch steps and opened our lunch boxes. I looked at her peanut butter sandwich with envy as I opened my tin lard bucket and took out my cold potato cake that lay with two cold biscuits.

Elizabeth was always saying that we were poor, and that she wished we had this, that, or the other. I wasn't sure what poor really meant, but I did wish that I could have a nice lunch box like Chester Aston, the boy we all thought was rich because he was an only child, and his folks owned a big farm, and they'd even been on trips out

West. Even Henry, my cousin, had a nice lunch box, but all I had was an old tin lard bucket.

I also often wished that I could have something really good to bring for my lunch. It seemed like we always had to bring the same old things -- fried green tomatoes in the fall and wormy apples that we'd picked up in the old orchard where the Phillips family used to live. In the winter after Daddy had butchered the two big sows we'd have fried tenderloin, or sausage as long as it lasted, and in the spring we were back to cold potato cakes made from leftover mashed potatoes, or maybe just a cold pancake. Mom often made cookies or homemade crackers, and we usually had an apple, pear, or in the fall bunches of small purple grapes that still grew on the old vines out in our orchard, but I longed for the "good lunches" that some of the others brought. Ellen sometimes had bologna sandwiches when her dad had been getting a lot of work, and some of the kids brought bananas, big red apples, bunches of huge red grapes, and even sometimes candy bars. We never had things like that, and neither did Ginny so I liked to eat lunch with her. She carried a tin lard bucket too. But she did sometimes have good things like peanut butter because her mother was a widow and people were always giving them things. I'd have liked to have had the things, but I didn't want my mother to be a widow for I'd just learned that that meant my daddy had to be dead and I didn't want that no way.

So, today as I looked longingly at the peanut butter sandwich, I said to Ginny, "I'll trade you this good potato cake for your peanut butter sandwich. You know how you like Mom's potato cakes when you come to stay overnight. Okay?"

Ginny was a year older than me and quite a bit bigger. Like me, she had dark curly hair, but she wore hers cut short, and mine always hung in long curls. Her eyes were gray green like mine and some people that didn't know any better thought we were sisters. She was good to me and usually gave in to my whims, but today she shook her head, and bit into the peanut butter sandwich eagerly.

"Sorry, Gin," (she was the only one that got by with calling me that), she said, "but Mr. Aston just brought this over last night, and I've been looking forward to it all morning." She took another bite and I felt mad at her. Seeing my frown, she added quickly, "I will trade you my cake for your cookies."

But this time I shook my head. Her cake looked more like bread than cake, and I knew Mom's chocolate cookies were good. I took the biscuits and potato cake up in my hands and began to eat. They tasted better than I had thought they would because I was hungry, but I did want that peanut butter.

That afternoon when we got home from school, me running most of the way ahead of Martha and Ellen who always walked so slowly, I ran down to the garden where Mom was planting some of the seeds that Joey had just received from the Seed Company that he sold them for to get prizes. At my call, she straightened up and rubbed her back as though she were very tired. But her smile was there as always.

"Hi, Ginny," she called. "How was school today?" She'd had to quit school in sixth grade because her papa didn't think education was important and they needed her at home, but she valued it highly and always wanted us to do our best. Martha had explained this to me last year when I grew weary of school and didn't want to go anymore. And everyday she asked each of us about our day as though she really cared.

"It was fine," I now answered. "We had a long lunch hour cause they were practicing for track. Ginny and I played Stink Base with the little kids." Then I got right to the point. "Mom, will you send for some peanut butter when Joey goes to town with Clifford on Saturday? Ginny had some for lunch today and I wanted it so much. Will you?"

My mother stood there for a few moments leaning on her hoe, looking down at me, then she wiped her dirt stained hand across her brow, and shook her head. "I'm sorry, Ginny," she said. "But we don't have enough money to buy peanut butter just now." Then seeing my look of unhappiness, she added, "We'll buy some next fall when we sell the corn crop," and went back to her planting.

Now, I knew what Elizabeth meant when she was always saying we were poor. That night I prayed that God would make us rich, or, at least, rich enough to buy peanut butter, but He didn't.

Joey hadn't been able to go to high school either because he had to take over the farm when Daddy was so sick, and now before he put in our crops in the spring, he hired himself out to the farmers nearby who had bigger farms. This spring he was working for a farmer over across the Little Wabash River. He'd been gone for two weeks and was due back this Saturday. Elizabeth had ridden with him on Star, our big reddish colored mare, to the river, then after he swam across, she rode home alone. She told me later that she'd been terribly frightened to ride so far by herself, but she had made it safely. So, on Saturday morning, she started out bravely to go meet him after Daddy helped her saddle Star.

Mom still couldn't afford to pay for the bus for Elizabeth to go to High School in Carmen, but she'd found her a ride with a neighbor down to Harrodville, a tiny community five miles south of us that consisted of a church, a store, a school, and several houses. An elderly schoolteacher had started his own little high school with only seven students, and Elizabeth was one of those lucky few. She was so happy at getting to further her education with the thought that someday she would be a great published poet that she was a more cheerful person than she had been before. She was singing as she set off down the road toward the river. I stood in the front yard waving after she'd told me that I couldn't go with her because Star couldn't carry all three of us back.

I was happy to see Joey when they returned because we always missed any member of the family when they were away, and also because I'd had to do many more chores while he was away. I was happier than ever to see him when he came back that afternoon from town with Clifford, our cousin's husband, who lived in the old

Haines's homeplace down the road from us, because he had spent part of his precious earnings to buy each of us girls a Payday candy bar. Elizabeth, Martha, and Janice all ate theirs right away, but I decided when I saw it that I would save it for my lunch on Monday. I hid it away in the old trunk in the bedroom, and several times before Monday, I slipped in there alone to hold it in my hand and sniff it. The aroma was wonderful! Maybe since God couldn't give me peanut butter, He'd at least given me a peanut candy bar! I could hardly wait until Monday.

Then when Naomi came out for a visit on Sunday afternoon, I thought my cup had surely runneth over for she brought a sack of goodies -- bologna, a loaf of light bread, some bananas, and even a bunch of big red grapes. She was always spending some of her hard earned small salary to bring us treats. But honest as always, she confided in us, "Uncle Tobias sent the fruit, but I bought the bologna and bread."

When Mom sat us down to divide up the treats, I surprised them all by saying, "Mom, I want to save all my share to take for my lunch Monday. Then with my candy bar, I'll have the best lunch ever. Oh, and can I have the paper sack too?" I couldn't bear to put this delicious lunch in that old lard bucket.

Mom seemed to understand. I guess she was remembering about the peanut butter. But she just nodded and handed me my banana and a small bunch of the grapes. "I'll put your bologna in the bucket with the milk and butter down in the cistern to keep it fresh for tomorrow," she said. We had no electricity so therefore no refrigerator, and that was how she kept our food from spoiling.

I said, "Thank you. I'll get me a glass of milk, and eat it with cornbread while you all eat that." It was hard looking at that food I wanted it so badly. Martha started to save some of hers, but she ended up eating it all so only I had the good stuff for tomorrow.

When I woke up the next morning, I felt very excited and at first couldn't figure out what it was all about. Then I remembered my special lunch. So, I sprang out of bed and dressed quickly. I took my candy bar from its secret hiding place and hurried to the kitchen. Mom was fixing breakfast, but she stopped long enough to hand me my sandwich wrapped in wax paper which she had brought in with the milk. Then she handed me the paper sack with my grapes and banana already in it as she said, "My, I wish I could be there to share your special lunch with you."

Suddenly I wished that she could be too, and I put my arms around her and hugged her hard. I put my sandwich and candy bar in the sack and folded down the top. Then I wrote my name in big letters—GINNY HAINES—on the sack with a pencil that lay on one end of the long table with my arithmetic book. I was so excited that I could hardly eat my breakfast.

When Martha and I got to school, I couldn't resist showing my wonderful lunch to Ginny and Ellen. Some of the boys crowded close to look too. When the teacher came out in the cloakroom where we kept our wraps and lunches, girls at one side and boys on the other, ringing the big handbell, I hurriedly stuck it at the back of the shelf and put some lunchbuckets in front of it.

We had reading and writing the first period so after I had read my story aloud for Mr. Grafton, I practiced making my capital letters while the older kids had history lessons. I think I learned to love history in those early days as I listened to them as they recited. But today I didn't listen very much for I kept thinking about that delicious lunch and daydreaming that I was rich and had those kind of lunches every day.

At recess, I took the sack down and looked hungrily at the food, but decided to save it all for lunch and put it back. I played hopscotch with Ginny and the little girls in first and second grade, and I won. This was my lucky day.

Second period was arithmetic time. After checking my assignment with the teacher, I worked on the new lesson and thought more and more about that lunch as the time drew nearer and nearer to enjoy it.

When we were dismissed for lunch, we all made a beeline to the pump outside except in very cold or rainy weather for Mr. Grafton insisted that we wash our hands before eating. So, as someone pumped we all stuck our hands under the cold water and, at least, got them wet. We dried them by waving them in the air, or wiping them on our clothes so it probably didn't do us any good to wash them in the first place.

Back in the cloakroom, there was a wild surge to grab the lunchbuckets or sacks. The taller bigger girls always managed to grab theirs first and dash for the outdoors. If it was cool, they sat in the sun, and if it were hot, they spread their lunches on the grass under the big old walnut trees at the edge of the playground.

Today, I just waited until they were gone, then I reached up to get my sack, and could not believe it when my hand came back empty. Unable to believe it, I stood on tiptoe and peered at the shelf. I couldn't see any sack. Ginny was waiting with her bucket by the big double doors that led to the porch. But seeing my predicament, she came back to help.

"Want me to reach it for you?" she asked. She was taller than me and often helped me in this way.

I said, "Yeah, please do. I can't reach it," but I already knew by the terrible feeling in the pit of my stomach that it was not there.

Ginny reached and stretched and stood on tiptoe, but she could see nothing. Her face showed her concern as she put her hand on my shoulder. "It's not here, honey."

"Maybe someone put it on the top shelf," I said in a low voice, but somehow I knew that wasn't true. My wonderful, delicious, mouth-watering lunch that I had thought constantly about since yesterday afternoon, even during church last night, was gone!

"I'll get a chair and look," she offered, and we dragged a chair from the classroom to look, but nothing was up there but some empty sacks. "Oh, honey, I'm sorry." She climbed down and put her arms around me. "Let's go tell Martha and Ellen. Maybe they took it out to the trees with them." I knew it wasn't true, but I followed her outside to the trees. When I saw Martha, I began to cry like I always do when things are very wrong and I see Martha.

GINNY'S DREAM

"Her lunch is gone," Ginny explained as Martha and Ellen looked up from the grass where they were eating with Betsy and Alma, Ginny's big sisters, who were in eighth grade.

"Not your delicious lunch!" exclaimed Martha getting to her feet and putting her arms around me.

I was sobbing by now so I just nodded my head and clung to her. "Somebody stole it," I finally blurted out between my sobs.

"Oh, no," they all answered in chorus. People just didn't steal in our school. We hid our prize possessions away when kids from other schools came for basketball games, or track meets for fear they would steal them, but not kids from our own school. Oh, maybe a pencil or eraser dropped on the floor might be picked up and used. But a lunch stolen from the cloakroom? Never.

"Maybe you didn't look good enough," suggested Ellen, but Ginny assured her that we had even to using a chair.

Then Alma insisted that we go tell the teacher, and gathering up their lunches we all trailed inside to tell Mr. Grafton about the theft. He seemed genuinely sorry and left his own lunch to go with us to all the places where the other students were eating. He questioned all of them, but no one seemed to know anything, and we could see that no one was eating my lunch. The girls all offered me part of their lunches, and even the teacher offered me some of his, but I was too upset to eat so I sat on the porch and cried until he rang the bell and I had to wash my face to go back inside.

I was so disappointed and angry and my head ached from crying and not having lunch that I spent a miserable afternoon. The teacher talked again to the kids about my lunch being taken, and I thought that someone would surely tell, but no one said a word. They didn't seem to know a thing.

Somehow, I got through my language and spelling classes and then it was recess again. When Martha pressed a cookie into my hands that she'd saved me from her lunch, I was so hungry that I took it. That helped to get me through health and science and then it was time to go home.

My eyes were still red and swollen from crying and my head still ached. I walked home silently with my head staring at the ground. That's probably why I saw the paper sack laying by the side of the road near the mailbox. I knew before I picked it up and saw my name that it was my stolen lunch. I was right, of course, and the banana peeling and candy wrapper were inside. But who had taken it and how had it gotten all that long way from the school?

We never found out for sure who had taken my special lunch that I had so looked forward to, but I suspected it was Bill Matthews for he walked home that way, and was always doing something to aggravate the girls, and I knew he was one of the boys looking when I proudly showed my lunch to Ellen and Ginny. Or, it could have been Henry, my cousin, because he was older and meaner, and I never really cared for him. Or, in my imaginative mind, it might have been a tramp who had sneaked into the cloakroom while we were all doing arithmetic, some at the board making a lot of noise, and stolen my lunch. But one thing I knew for certain was that if I had brought it in my old tin lard bucket instead of the sack, it probably wouldn't have been stolen as the bucket would have been harder to conceal than the sack. I had learned a hard lesson early in life. As my mother often told us her grandma had always said, "Pride cometh before a fall." And I had really fallen!

Chapter 4

Bucket of Honey

W e got out of school the first week in May so the bigger boys could help with the spring planting, and so, I supposed, that the teachers could get their crops in too. Even though I loved school very much, it was good to be out and to have the long summer months to look forward to. I loved the outdoors and spent as much time as possible after my chores were done wandering through the fields down to the bluffs and creek, or playing in the hayloft that covered most of our big barn.

I liked to imagine or pretend things, and my imaginary playmate that summer I was eight was named Mary, and she shared all of my adventures. We were Indian maidens living in tepees down by the creek, gathering wild berries from the bushes and fish from the creek for our food. In the hayloft, we were usually famous actresses putting on radio shows where I did all the parts including the men. I also did this when I walked to and from our mailbox, back to the creek, or picked dewberries in the field across from our orchard. I made up my own script as I went along, talking to myself as I played all the parts. I dreamed of becoming a famous author who would write books and plays and radio scripts. I would travel all over, and everyone would know me, and I could eat peanut butter and grapes and bananas and candy bars and even bologna every day if I wanted to.

Janice was four now and she liked to tag along with me. Of course, I couldn't do my shows when she was along, but sometimes I felt sorry for her and took her with me. She was little and quick and could keep up with me even when I walked my fastest. Her blonde hair was longer now and Mom had begun to braid it in two plaits that hung down her back. They bounced as she ran along beside me her blue eyes sparkling.

Often with her, I built playhouses under the grove of plum trees using old pieces of broken furniture, dishes and pans, and using long sticks as the walls. After it rained, we gathered mud from the dirt road in front of our house, and made mud pies, cookies, cakes, and suckers on sticks. After laying them in the sun, they would become hard and could be used for several days. Ellen, who was now eleven, still liked to play in the playhouses, and she often joined us. Martha played this with us too, but her favorite games were "Hoopy Hide", or "May I?"

Another one of our fun things was walking the three miles straight south of us down past Ellen's house, and on past her grandma's house that had burned down, and all the way across the big gravel road where we had to look carefully for cars, and then down a little lane by a big woods to the other Ginny's house to stay all day.

On a hot day in early July, Martha, Ellen, and I had planned to go. We had made plans with Ginny, Alma, and Betsy on Sunday morning at Sunday School, and it had been cleared by all our mothers. But when Tuesday morning came, and I was all excited about going, Martha woke up with a cold and a sore throat, and Mom said that she couldn't go. I was afraid that she wouldn't let me go either, so I got up and dressed quickly, and hurried into the kitchen to plead my case.

Mom had Alice tied in the rocking chair feeding her oatmeal because she never had a high chair for any of her babies, and when she saw me, she said, "Oh, Ginny, would you finish feeding Alice while I go fix a rag with some Vicks on it to put around Martha's throat? And see that Janice finishes her oatmeal too." Janice was perched on her knees at the long table spooning the food into her mouth.

I started to say, "Why can't Elizabeth do this?" But Mom was gone and the bowl and spoon were in my hands. Then I remembered that Elizabeth had gone early this morning before the sun got too hot with Daddy back in the field to pick blackberries. I decided that if I helped now that Mom would still let me go. So, I began to persuade in my most impressive voice, "Come on, Alice, open your mouth and eat this good warm oatmeal." And to my surprise, she did just that.

Alice was a cute little tyke with Naomi's brown eyes and Martha's red hair, but hers lay in little ringlets all over her head. I liked to hold her and play with her, but I didn't want to be responsible for her any length of time.

By the time I had finished feeding her, Janice had finished her bowl and was asking for more. I was spooning it out of the pan on the back of the big wood range into her bowl when my mother came back into the kitchen.

"Thanks, Ginny," she said. "You'd better eat some yourself so you can get on your way, or Ellen will wonder what has happened to you."

"You mean I can go even though Martha is sick?" I asked in amazement realizing that I wasn't even going to have to beg.

Mom smiled as she took the bowl from me to hand to Janice. "I don't see why not. You've walked to Ellen's enough times alone, and she'll be going the rest of the way with you. Just make sure you get home before dark." Then she dished me a bowl of oatmeal and handed me a glass of warm milk.

As soon as I had eaten, I went outside to brush my teeth using a big glass of cold water to rinse out my mouth and then spit it out on the grass. In the wintertime, we had to spit into a washpan in the kitchen, and then empty it outside as we had no indoor plumbing.

I went back to the kitchen to leave the glass, kiss my mother good-by, and promise again to be back before dark, and then I ran out the back door, and took off down the road to Ellen's house. It was a quarter of a mile so I had time to do part of my radio play on the way.

Ellen was waiting for me down by our mailboxes for she had gotten ready early and come to meet us. She was dressed as I was in a simple cotton dress though her mother had made hers and mine came from the Relief Barrel -- another reason why Elizabeth complained that we were poor. As usual, we were both barefooted.

"Hi, Ginny," she called as I came up to her. "Where's Martha? Isn't she going?"

"Hi, Ellen," I replied. "No, she's sick with a cold and sore throat and Mom made her stay in bed."

"But she let you come," she said in surprise. "I'd have thought she would have made you stay home too."

I smiled and felt important. "No, she said that I could come with you, but I must be home before dark."

"No problem there," she answered. "Let's get started for it's a long walk."

I nodded and we began to climb the long hill that led up to where her dad was building their new house. While it was being built, they slept in the big barn that he had built earlier, and cooked and ate in the smokehouse. I loved to stay all night there for it was exciting to sleep in the barn. They only had one milk cow that stayed in a shed out back and some chickens in the chicken house so the barn was like a big open house. My daddy still used horses for plowing and planting, but her dad who worked on cars and trucks when he wasn't farming, already had a small John Deere tractor.

Her mother was making beds out in the barn with Grandma Whitfield sitting down watching her. Ellen's aunt and uncle lived with them too and she had two little brothers, Victor, a year younger than me and Burt, the same age as Janice, so she had a big family too. Her mother's name was Milly, and she was one of my favorite people. She was always laughing and smiling and seemed pleased to see us when we visited. I loved to hear her sing, and often begged her to sing "The Miner's Child," but it was a sad song and always made Ellen cry. Now, she greeted me, asked about Martha, reminded us as my mother had that we were to be home before dark, and sent us on our way. Grandma Whitfield smiled and waved, but she didn't talk much anymore and some days didn't even get out of bed.

Soon, we were on our way skipping down the old dirt road that led to Grandma Whitfield's place where they'd all lived before the house burned. Mom and us girls had stood at the front window watching the blaze while Daddy and Joey had gone down to help fight the fire, but there was nothing they could do by carrying buckets of water from the well, or beating it with wet tow sacks.

When we came to the burned down house, we stopped for awhile, leaning on the old rickety gate that led to the barnyard. The old barn still stood there, unused and vacant, and the blackened ruins of the house still lay as they had fallen. Her dad felt it was more important to get the new house done before cold weather, and then he'd work on this. I wondered if he'd ever clean it up for no one saw it and who would care?

Soon Ellen said, "Let's go," and we took off on the worst part of the trip. From there to the gravel road we had just a narrow path through tall weeds that was over a mile long. We didn't like this part of the walk, but it saved so much time not going up to the schoolhouse and then all the way around by the gravel road which added about two miles. So, with her in the lead, we took off hoping that there were no snakes or lizards in the weeds. We laughed and talked, and even sang some songs we'd learned at church, "The Lily of the Valley" and "I Come to the Garden Alone" which we sang most every Sunday. I guess we thought God would keep the snakes away if we sang His songs.

But when Ellen stopped suddenly, so suddenly that she stepped down hard on my bare feet, and gave a loud scream, I knew we were in trouble. She turned around to face me and began pushing me back down the path, and now I could understand her screams, "There's a snake, a snake, a snake right in the path, and I almost stepped on it with my bare feet."

We ran backwards until we felt we were safe then we cautiously crept forward again with our eyes wide open and our hearts racing. Of all of God's creatures, snakes were the most fearsome to us. I certainly agreed with what my mother said that her grandma used to say, "I wish God had not had Noah take snakes on the ark, and then there wouldn't be any." I know they eat mice and insects, but I still don't like them.

Suddenly we could see the snake again, and we stopped dead still staring at it. It lay in the middle of the path as though it were asleep. It did not have its head up and its wicked little tongue darting in and out like they did when they were frightened, but it was a big black snake and looked so frightening. What were we to do? We were afraid to go out in the weeds in case there were more that we couldn't see, and we certainly couldn't walk down that path with that monster lying there in the way.

"Maybe if we wait a little while, it'll go away," I whispered as though I were afraid the snake would hear and know our plan.

But Ellen shook her head as though she didn't believe that at all. "If we had some rocks, we could throw them at it, but we don't have any rocks."

"Yeah, if we had a hoe, we could chop its head off like Mom does," I added for Mom hated snakes as much or maybe more than I did and I guess I got my fear from her.

"You could chop its head off. Not me." Ellen stepped back and put her arm around my shoulder.

We waited and waited, and finally I said, "Well, shall we just go home? We can't stand here all day."

And then as though he heard me and wanted to be obliging, that big old snake just turned and crawled off into the weeds. We looked at each other as though we could not believe it.

"Let's go," said Ellen grabbing my hand, "But let's run until we're far past that spot.

I nodded and we ran, first Ellen and then me running as fast as we could go, not stopping until we reached the gravel road. Hot, flushed faced and panting, we stopped and caught our breath before we went on up the little lane past the trees that were so many they were called a woods until we reached the Harper home.

I loved that house! It was a brick house with an upstairs and a basement. It had a long front porch with concrete steps with a concrete seat at each side where you could sit when you were tired. Inside there was a long living room all across the front of the house with a fireplace at one end and bookcases full of books on each side of the fireplace, then back from the left was a dining room with a big round table, and behind that the kitchen where they had a sink with a little pump to get water and a big bucket underneath to catch the water for they had no indoor plumbing either. Back from the right of the living room, there were three big bedrooms and one real little bedroom where Ginny slept and which years later would become the bathroom. Then between the back bedroom and the kitchen there were steps that went upstairs to the two bedrooms, and steps that went downstairs to the basement where they had a real furnace. So, they had no heating stove in their living room. It was a big house with lots of rooms, but I guess they needed it with ten children, even though the five older ones were all married, or working away from home. I loved that house, and fantasized that it was mine, and that I was a famous author, and could eat what I wanted to every day.

Ginny and Rex were waiting for us on the front steps when we came hurrying across the yard.

"You're late," said Rex.

"Where's Martha?" asked Betsy coming out on the front porch.

But all we could say was, "We saw a big black snake and we nearly stepped on it and we need a drink of water bad."

Rex laughed at us for being afraid of an old snake, but Ginny's eyes showed concern, and gentle kind Betsy took us into the kitchen for a drink of cold water and even a cold wet washrag to wipe our faces. After than, we began to calm down and feel better.

Alma, at thirteen and the oldest girl at home, was in the kitchen cooking dinner. In the country in those days of the late thirties, farmers always had dinner in the middle of the day and a light supper in the evening. She was cutting up pieces of potatoes into a big pot of green beans fresh from the garden that was cooking in a big pot on the wood burning stove. I could see pieces of onion and bacon simmering in the pot, and I felt very hungry. When she finished that, she took a big crock of cornbread batter and poured it into a huge black baking tin that set on the back of the range glistening with melted lard. Then she opened the oven door and shoved the pan inside. Finally, she turned to us to say hello and to ask about Martha.

Betsy explained to her about the snake and about Martha being sick as we had told her on our way to the kitchen. Alma was a very practical person who worked hard to help her mother as did all the children. I always thought we had a lot of chores to do until I went there and saw all they did. Why, they cleaned all the house, did the laundry with a washtub and wash board, planted and cared for the garden, mowed the grass, fed the animals, milked the cows, and even put in and harvested the crops. It seemed they couldn't do enough to help their mother who made all their clothes and did most of the cooking. They certainly loved her very much.

Alma said, "Well, it looks like we will have a lot to eat for Peter is eating over at Andrews's house, and Martha is sick, and Mama had to go to Minnie's as the baby is sick." Minnie was their older sister who was married and lived near them. "Hope you're hungry."

"I surely am," I replied, "And I love what you're cooking. Green beans and cornbread are two of my favorite things." This was really true and I was not just trying to be nice.

Ellen agreed with me and asked if we could help. But Alma said, "No, thanks," and then added, "Why don't you all go start your ball game, and I'll call you when it's ready?"

"Yeah, let's go," cried Rex who was standing in the doorway with Ginny. "I've got the bases all laid out under the trees."

So, we all trooped outside to start our ball game. It was a treat to play here for Rex had a real softball and bat that his older sister who worked in St. Louis had bought him while we still played with an old rubber ball that was falling apart and a stick for a bat. I thought again that except for not having a daddy which I wouldn't like, these kids sure had it made.

We were hot and thirsty again by the time Alma called us in to dinner so we washed our hands and faces at the sink, and drank big dippers of cold water. Then we trooped into the table and found a place. Besides the food already mentioned, there were fresh pickled beets and pickles from the garden as well as round red and long white icicle radishes, big glasses of cold milk, and even apple pie that Betsy had made that morning. Those girls sure were good cooks.

Before we ate, Alma had us to hold hands while she said the blessing. She was already a Christian and even taught the little kids in Sunday School.

The meal was delicious, and when we were done Betsy washed the dishes, Ellen and I dried them, and Ginny put them away and swept the kitchen. Then Alma joined us and we finished our ball game. After that Rex wandered off, and we girls sat on the front porch and talked and played some games of "Old Maid". We had finished our sixth game and I had just won, having been able to successfully pass the Old Maid card to unsuspecting Betsy, when Alex came running across the front yard yelling, "I've found a beetree in the woods, and the hive is low enough that we can get the honey. Come and help me!"

We all jumped to our feet excited and eager to go except Alma, who as the eldest, showed caution. "But the bees are sure to be there," she cautioned, "And we're sure to get stung."

"We don't know how to get honey out of a hive," agreed Betsy who was twelve and usually followed her older sister's advice. "And I don't know what Mama would s—"

But Rex was not to be discouraged. "I didn't see any bees. They're probably all asleep. Besides, I've got it all figured out. We'll put on some old pants and sweaters and we'll put paper sacks over our heads with the eyes cut out like we do on Halloween. There won't be anything left to sting but our hands and feet, and we'll do it so fast those old bees won't know what hit them."

His enthusiasm caught us all, even the older girls, and we ran for the basement where the old clothes were kept and soon we were all dressed in outrageous outfits. Betsy found some big paper sacks and cut out eyes for each of us. These we carried in our hands until we got near the bee tree. Rex warned us to be quiet, so we followed him single file through the woods with our fingers to our lips. None of us thought of the consequences, only the reward which would be barrels of honey. "Maybe, we'll even have enough to sell," I thought.

Suddenly, Rex stopped and pointed ahead. We could all see the tall hickory nut tree with the huge beehive about half way up. He put his sack over his head and the rest of us followed suit. "I think I can knock it down," he whispered. "I'll climb up the tree and try. If it falls, grab it and run before the bees come back."

We watched as he scurried up the tree, his bare feet wrapping around the trunk as he went. He climbed until he was close enough to touch it then he began to push with all his might. But quickly as though it were an enemy scout, a single bee flew from behind the hive and as quickly stung him on the hand. He let out a yowl and slid down the tree. Instinctively, we all drew back expecting a whole swarm of bees, but none came so we moved in closer again.

"Let's try knocking it down with long sticks," suggested Ginny, and since this seemed like a good idea we all scattered looking for sticks minus our masks. When we'd found ones we thought would be suitable, we reassembled at the base of the tree and donned our masks. Then we began to beat and pound the hive. For awhile nothing happened, then they came so quickly we hardly knew what hit us. The bees swarmed all about us, stinging our hands and feet and even flying up under the sacks to sting our faces. Yelling and screaming, we began to run with someone yelling, "Retreat, retreat."

Halfway back to the house we stopped to lick our wounds. Fortunately, none of us were allergic to bee stings so except for itching and burning no one was too badly hurt, but we all realized that no way were we going to get any honey doing what we had been doing. We were still standing there looking at each other in dismay, when Peter, their older brother, and his friend Jack Andrews, who was in Martha and Ellen's grade at school, came charging through the woods. They stopped and stared at us in amazement. After we told our story, first they laughed; then they offered to help.

Peter sent Rex back to the house for some matches and some old rags. Then they took Alma and Betsy's outfits and masks, and when Rex returned they took the matches and rags and went to the bee tree with us following fearfully along behind. Again, the bees seemed to be gone so the boys lit the matches, set fire to the old rags which smouldered and smoked as they wanted them to instead of burning, and climbed the trees, one on either side of the bee tree. Then they reached out to the hive with the smoking rags time and again until finally the bees flew out and instead of stinging them, they all flew away. We stood and stared in disbelief. Then they hit with all their force knocking the hive to the ground.

Forgetting our fear, we all dashed over as Peter kicked it over exposing the honeycomb where the honey was stored. It wasn't barrels and there wouldn't be any to sell, but it was honey, and we all felt like true pioneers.

Peter carried it to the back porch for fear the bees would come back, and Alma went inside to get a bowl to put the honey in. It was Ginny who said, "We have to give Ellen and Ginny some for they helped too."

And Rex added, "And Jack gets some for he really helped."

So, Alma went back inside and brought back four of the tin lard buckets that we all used for lunch buckets. Then she spooned some of the golden rich honey in each of the buckets and put the lids on tightly.

It was Betsy who suddenly exclaimed, "My goodness, the sun is setting. I had no idea it was so late." And turning to Ellen and me she added, "You two had better get started, or it will be dark before you get home."

We hadn't realized how late it was either. Hastily, we grabbed our buckets of honey, said thanks and good-byes and started up the road. Neither of us wanted to take the path through the weeds with that snake lurking out there probably waiting for us, but we knew we had no choice.

We had no time to go the long way so bravely we struck out up the path. I tried to pray that there'd be no snakes, but I had a feeling that God was displeased with me for disobeying my mother, and I kept hoping the honey would so please her that she wouldn't be mad. She was usually very calm, but sometimes, as my daddy said, she got her red-headed dander up and really got angry.

We didn't say much as we hurried up that path, past the old farmstead, and on up to Ellen's new house. God was good and kept the snake away, but it kept getting darker and darker. It had been twilight when we left Harpers' house, and it was almost completely dark now. No way could I get home before dark.

Milly was standing on top of the hill straining her eyes as she watched for us. "Where in the world have you been?" she asked her anxiety showing in her voice.

Ellen began to explain to her about the bee tree while she stared at us in amazement. Then she turned to me. "Want me to walk you home, Ginny? It's almost dark."

"No," I answered bravely. "I'll be all right, but thanks anyway." And clutching my little bucket of honey I trudged on toward home hoping every step of the way that Mom would forgive me when she saw the delicious honey.

I had just reached the mailbox when I saw a tall dark figure coming down our road. Before I could get frightened, I heard Elizabeth's voice calling, "Ginny, is that you?"

"Yes, Elizabeth," I answered happily as I ran to her thankful that she had come for I really didn't like walking in the dark alone.

"Why are you so late?" she asked as I reached her and took her hand. "And what in the world do you have?" as she noticed the bucket clutched tightly in my right hand.

"We found a beetree," I said excitedly, "And we tried to get the honey and we got stung even under our masks then Peter and Jack came and smoked them out and we got some honey. I've got a bucket full of honey."

Elizabeth laughed. "Well, I hope Mom buys that story."

"Is she awful mad?"

"No, just worried."

And that made me feel worse for I hated worrying Mom for she had enough to worry about anyway.

When we reached home, it was Daddy who saved the day for when he saw the honey, he was delighted as he loved sweet things to put on his hot biscuits for breakfast. I saw him smile at her and shake his head warningly even as I hugged her to say I was sorry. The bucket of honey had spared me a scolding after all.

Chapter 5

Big Ditches

One of our favorite places to play was what we called the Big Ditches. It was in the field across the road from our orchard belonging to the farm where the Bates family lived. It was really some huge gullies that had been washed away by the rains over the years, but we always called them the Big Ditches, and it was a magical place to play.

They were so deep that we had to climb down inside them. It was like a huge circle with points that jutted out so that we could easily imagine that they were walls between rooms. Usually we pretended that it was a big castle and that we lived in it. It was always a battle of who would get to be the king or queen. But sometimes it became a stable for our stick horses that we had ridden across the prairie whether we were just cowboys or vicious outlaws hiding there from the sheriff's posse.

Sometimes Ginny and Rex joined us, but usually it was just Martha, Ellen, Victor, and I. We spent long hours playing there, and if either of our parents wanted us, they usually knew where to look.

The week after our triumph over the bees, Ellen and Victor came up one afternoon bringing four year old Burt with them. When we decided to go play at the Big Ditches, Janice demanded to go along since Burt was going so we had to give in. We took a jar of cold water with us and Mom gave us a bag of fresh baked chocolate drop cookies which was one of our favorite treats. This would be our feast in the castle. We waved good-by and set off down through the orchard. Some green apples were on the ground so we picked them up to add to our feast. Before we reached the Big Ditches, Victor had proclaimed that he was going to be king that day, and for once no one protested. Usually, Ellen or Martha claimed that since they were the oldest that they got to be queen.

Little Janice piped up, "If he's the king, then I get to be a princess."

And Burt said that he'd be the prince. So, Victor, getting back at the older girls, declared that they would be the servants, but I could be his queen. Ellen and Martha were both in a good mood and they presented no argument. So, looking forward to the day's fun, we arrived at the castle.

Martha and Ellen climbed down first and then helped Janice and Burt down. Victor and I scrambled down by ourselves. We went first to the room that we had long ago designated as the kitchen, whether it was a castle or a ranchhouse, and left our food and water there.

Then we returned to the big room that was always our throne room, and we spent some time building back the thrones with the rocks that had fallen over. Finally, when they were finished, Victor and I sat on them as though we were really the king and queen with Janice and Burt standing behind us while we gave orders to the servants.

Soon, we were tired of this and Victor took Burt away on a hunting trip while we cleaned the castle and got the food ready for their return. We gathered soft dead grass to make beds in the various rooms which were separated by the walls of the pointed parts of the gully that stretched high above our heads. Then we went to the kitchen to lay out the food for the hunters' return. When they came scrambling down the banks, hot and tired, we all took drinks of the cold water from the jar and ate most of the cookies and apples.

When we were finished, Victor stood up and announced, "I'm going to go exploring. Anyone want to go along?"

"No, we're going to take our afternoon naps," replied Martha for all of us, no longer a servant, but now a Lady in Waiting, or something. She stood up and stretched as though she were very tired. "Come along, girls, it's time for our beauty rest." Martha didn't always play with us, but when she did she made the most of it.

We all rose to follow her, and even little Burt said, "I'm tired. I want a nap," and he trailed off after Ellen to share her bed of leaves. So, Victor climbed back up the steep cliff and took off on his own pretending that he was really a king surveying his kingdom.

"I want to sleep with you," said Janice taking Martha's hand. "I don't want my own castle room."

"Then we made up an extra bed for nothing," I grumbled, but good natured Martha just smiled and led her to her bedroom. Then, I set off down the long corridor to the room I had chosen at the far end. Once there and still pretending that I was the queen, I stood quietly while my servants helped me off with my royal robes before I lay down on my royal bed to rest. None of us really intended to sleep, but it was all part of the game.

But I must have dozed off for suddenly I heard a scream and the sound of something falling, and I was instantly on my feet and running toward the sound. But as I rounded a corner and could see into a crevice that was not visable on the way down, I braked to a sudden stop while my heart pounded loudly for there lying inside the crevice was a man with his head resting on a bundle of clothes or rags sound asleep.

I assumed that he must be a tramp. That's what we called the men who were out of work and who tramped about the country carrying all their belongings tied up in a pack on their backs. Sometimes they rode the freight trains, and got off at Applesville to look for work, or to beg for food. Sometimes they came to our back door and Mom gave them whatever leftovers we had which usually wasn't very much, or she'd fix them a cup of coffee. They'd usually chop some wood, or do some chore to pay for the food, and I had talked to them either as they ate or worked. Therefore, I was not afraid of them, but somehow the sudden appearance of this man in our castle seemed like an intrusion, and I was afraid.

But before I could decide what to do, I heard another cry and then Martha calling me urgently so I set off running toward the sound of her voice. When I rounded the bend and came to the place where we always climbed down into the ditches, I saw Victor lying on the ground in a strange position with his right arm flung out, and he was crying something awful. No longer was he the mighty king of a few minutes ago, but a frightened and hurting little boy. The others stood grouped around him showing their fear on their faces except for Martha who knelt on the ground beside him, cradling his head in her hands. All the playacting was over and she was again calm practical Martha who always seemed to know what to do. As I came closer, I could see the reason for all the concern. Victor's arm was broken and the bone was pushing through the flesh. It looked gross. I didn't even ask what had happened for I knew that he had fallen down the cliff and this was the result. My first thought was, "We'll never get to come play here again," and I felt sad.

Now, Martha was giving orders. "Ellen, you run to your house as fast as you can, and get your dad. Tell him to hurry," she shouted as Ellen climbed up the slope and took off running. We didn't have a phone so that was probably the fastest way to get help.

Then she turned to me. "Ginny, you take Burt and Janice to our house and tell Mom. Maybe she'll know what to do. Do be careful getting them up the bank." When I hesitated, she grew cross, "Ginny, do as I say. Go."

"But, Martha, there's a t—"

"Oh, Ginny, stop thinking up excuses and take them now."

Then I looked at the two little ones and saw that they were both crying.

Victor had quit screaming and lay with his eyes closed moaning softly. His face was white and he seemed to be stunned.

Hoping that the tramp would stay asleep and not hurt Martha and Victor, I took Burt's hand and half pulled, half pushed him up the bank to solid ground. Then ordering him to stay there, I went back for Janice. She was crying harder and didn't want to leave Martha, but I was bigger and stronger so I dragged her up out of the ditches. I took Burt's hand and ran with them back across the field, through our orchard, and up to our yard.

"Mom," I yelled. "Mom, come quick," and when she stuck her head out the passageway between the kitchen and the smokehouse, I said quickly, "Victor fell down the bank and broke his arm and the bone is sticking out and Ellen's gone to get her dad and Martha is staying with him and there's a tr—" but I decided quickly to not tell her that part so added "I've got to go back and help Martha so you keep Burt and Janice here."

By that time, she had stepped down into the yard and came over to where we were. Janice immediately flung herself into her arms sobbing wildly, and Burt began to cry again too. Mom knelt on the grass and took them both in her arms. Now, she had found her voice and looking up at me, said, "Ginny, you stay here with the little ones and I'll go help Martha."

But I shook my head determinedly, my dark curls bouncing. Somehow, I felt in my eight year old bravery that I needed to protect both Martha and my mother from the tramp asleep in the Big Ditches. Before she could change her suggestion to a command, I took off down through the orchard running. I ran all the way so slid down the bank hot and tired, not taking time to worry about hurting myself.

Martha had moved to a sitting position and had put Victor's head in her lap. His eyes were still closed and his face was whiter than ever. She put her fingers up to her lips as I came up beside her. "I do hope his dad is home," was all she said. Her red hair was cut in a short bob straight as a stick as Naomi was always saying. Martha's hair had been curly like mine until when she was about three years old, she had taken Mom's big scissors one day when she happened to be on the back porch alone and snipped off her curls. Mom had cried when she took her down to Milly's for Aunt Isabel to even it up. It ended up in a short bob and it was never curly again. Now, she flipped her head to get her hair out of her eyes and looked at me.

"Martha," I whispered. "There's a tramp asleep back there in the castle," I indicated with my head the direction from which I had come earlier. "I saw him when I left my bedroom. There's a tramp in our castle."

Alarm shown in Martha's green eyes. "Why didn't you tell me before you left me here alone?"

"I tried to," I answered, "But you told me to go on and take Burt and Janice home. Remember? I—"

"Yes, now I remember. Well, what shall we do?"

My big sister was asking me, "What do we do?"

"I came back to protect you and Victor instead of letting Mom come."

Martha smiled and took my hand in hers. "If we're real quiet, maybe he won't wake up," she whispered.

And I nodded my head. But I was still afraid that his being there and Victor getting hurt might keep us from getting to play there in our favorite place.

Suddenly, we heard the sound of a motor coming right across the field, and when I climbed up to the top, I saw Ellen's dad, Ethan Haas, driving his old red truck right up to the rim of the Big Ditches. Milly was in the front seat with him and she jumped out before the motor was switched off and came running over to me. Ellen leaped out of the back and came running too while Ethan came from the driver's side of the pickup.

"How is he?" asked Milly as she began to climb down the steep bank.

"He's awfully white and still," I answered not realizing that my words struck terror to her heart.

I never saw grownups get down a bank so quickly. When they saw Martha with Victor's head in her lap, they ran to him quickly. Milly began to cry when she saw the bone sticking out, but Ethan just stooped and took his son in his arms and began to cautiously climb to the top.

Then Ellen and I helped Milly back to the top while Martha stood up from her cramped position and stretched her arms and legs. Milly called to Ellen as they drove away with her holding Victor on her lap.

"Get Burt and go on home. We'll be back as soon as we can." Then she held Victor closer as he looked up at her and began to cry.

As soon as they were gone, Ellen said, "Guess I better go get Burt and go on home." Her flushed face was steaked with tears, and she was still hot and tired from her long run.

"Wait, Ellen," I said in a low voice. "You've got to come back down in the ditches with me first."

"Why?"

I leaned over and whispered in her ear. "Because there is a tramp asleep down there, and we've got to make sure Martha gets out safely."

"A tramp in our castle?" I didn't think she believed me so I tugged on her arm and pulled her over to the edge. Martha was standing there motioning us to come on down. So, very carefully for we didn't want any bones sticking out of our skin, we went back to the bottom.

"Let's go back to the kitchen to get our things," Martha said in a very low voice. "Then let's get out of here." We were always careful to keep the place clean and not leave any litter behind.

So, we crept silently back up the hallway to the kitchen, gathered up our sack and jar, and started back to the way to climb out. Suddenly, a voice behind us made us freeze in our steps and the hairs on the back of our necks bristled.

"What are you doing down here?" The voice was rough and coarse, and as we turned to look at him, it seemed that our hearts would pound right out of our bodies. Now, that he was on his feet instead of lying down asleep, I could see that he was a big man with an unkempt, dirty beard and moustache and wearing the dirtiest clothes I had ever seen. As he moved a step closer to us, I finally found my voice.

"We just play down here and pretend it's a castle," I spoke up boldly, angry that he had invaded our private place.

Martha, sensing my anger, said quickly, "We're leaving now, and we won't bother you anymore." And to me and Ellen, "Let's go." But as we started to go, he held out his hand.

"What's in the jar?"

"Water," Martha answered. "Just water."

"I want it. I'm thirsty." He took a step nearer and we backed a step farther away. "Give me the jar."

"Sure," said Martha handing him the jar and thinking to herself as she told us later, "The Bible says to give a cup of cold water in My name so Mom won't mind me giving away her jar as she tries to do what the Bible says." Then she pushed us ahead again.

But the man's voice stopped us again. "What's in the sack?"

"Just some apple cores and cookie crumbs," I replied not wanting to give the rest of our cookies to this hateful old man.

"Let me see," he held out his hand and grudgingly I gave it to him. He opened the sack and took out the one apple and the two or three cookies that were left then dumped the cores and crumbs on the ground throwing the sack down too. As he began to eat, we turned and ran.

Ellen and I didn't want to tell our parents for fear they wouldn't let us go back there to play, but honest Martha would not hear of it, and told Mom as soon as we got home. Later when Daddy and Joey came in from the fields, they went over to the Big Ditches to see what was going on. But the tramp and his clothes were gone. Only the mess he had made on the hall floor was there.

True to my fears, they wouldn't let us go there to play for a long time, but no more tramps were seen around there, and Victor's arm finally healed, so we were allowed to go back. But somehow, the accident and the tramp coming to our special place had spoiled the specialness for us, and we never enjoyed it quite as much. Years later our Big Ditches were bulldozed up and made into a pond for swimming, but I could never bring myself to go there. I wanted to remember the Big Ditches as they had been when I was a child and they were my castle.

Chapter 6

Traditions

That fall I started fourth grade. We had a new teacher by the name of Gordon Cross, but he wasn't cross at all. He was young as he'd just finished his required hours at the University so he could teach, and ours was his first school. Mr. Grafton had accepted a school nearer his home, and we supposed that he got more money than the $75.00 a month that our school paid for teaching all eight grades, being coach and janitor, for the teacher also had to sweep the floor and fire the furnace. At first, we were all very disappointed that he wasn't coming back, but we soon liked Mr. Cross for he was lots of fun and not too strict, and he, like Mr. Grafton, seemed to enjoy playing games with us. He also had a crush on Elizabeth, who was now in her second year of high school, so he was especially nice to Martha and me.

GINNY'S DREAM

I loved school so I was happy to get back to the studies, but it was also good to see all of my friends again, and to join in the ballgames or the big group games we played. We also had a new swing set of four swings so we didn't all have to fight over the one long rope swing that hung from a tallest branch of the old walnut tree that stood down near the girls' outside toilet. But the thing that I probably loved the most was the new teeter totter that had come with the swing set, and I always joined the wild rush for it when we were let out for recess. But I didn't very often win. Gradually, the interest wore off, however, and the older kids returned to their old games, or playing softball, and we could play on the teeter totter anytime we wanted. It was such fun to go up and down, up and down, and since I usually did it with the other Ginny, and even though she was bigger than I was, she was always careful not to make me bump hard on the ground so I thoroughly enjoyed it.

That fall we also got electricity in our school building so we were all excited about that even though it did mean that we could no longer put away our books and play games when a storm came up and it got too dark to study. We also got electricity in our church, and all the people who lived on or near the gravel road got it connected to their houses, but we didn't have it at our house for many long years.

As sunny September turned into the beautiful hues of October and the leaves turned red, orange, yellow, and brown, we began to pester Mr. Cross about planning for our annual community-wide wiener roast that was always held out behind the schoolhouse some evening in the fall. Since Martha and Ellen were the oldest girls in school, as there was no one in eighth grade that year, we unofficially appointed them to be the spokesmen for us.

Therefore, they stayed in one recess when the rest of us rushed out to play. But when we realized what they were doing, Ginny, the little girls, and I crept back into the cloakroom to listen.

Martha, as usual, took the initiative. "Mr. Cross," she said in her most grown up voice. "Do you know about the big wiener roast that we have every fall here at school?"

"No, I'm afraid that I don't," he answered. Even though he grew up in a community near ours, I guessed that they hadn't done that there. "Is it an annual tradition?"

"Oh, yes," chimed in Ellen. "We do it every year and everyone in the community comes and we all have such a wonderful time."

"And you buy the hot dogs and buns and marshmallows and mustard and catsup and everything and—" continued Martha.

"Wait a minute," interrupted the teacher. "I buy everything?" I guess he was trying to figure out how his $75.00 a month was going to buy all that and pay his bills too. So, I pushed ahead of the other girls hidden in the cloakroom and rushed into the classroom.

"No, Mr. Cross," I blurted out. "You buy them, but you don't pay for them."

"Now, wait a minute. Just how do I manage that?" He really seemed confused so I decided to straighten him out.

"Well," I explained while Martha glared at me for taking over. "You take the money from the box supper and bu—"

"What box supper?" he demanded.

"The one we have before we have the wiener roast" explained the other Ginny pushing up to the circle.

"Don't you know what a box supper is?" asked Ellen beginning to feel his puzzlement.

"Oh, yes, I know what a box supper is. When are we supposed to have that?"

"Right away," answered Martha, "Because we have to have the wiener roast before the weather turns bad."

"We all go out in the woods behind the school one afternoon and we drag in all the branches and pieces of dead wood that we can carry and we make a big stack for the biggest bonfire you ever saw," put in Ginny.

But Mr. Cross was still thinking of the box supper. "Will the highschoolers come to the box supper too?" he asked.

"Of course, they will," I answered and added with an impish grin before I turned and ran from the room, "Yes, Elizabeth will be there." I saw him blush before he turned to ask them more about the wiener roast.

Martha was staying that school year with an elderly lady that we all called Aunt Lucy. It was because she had rented a spare bedroom to an elderly gentleman, who we called Uncle Jake, and she didn't want the neighborhood to talk about the two of them living together. Elizabeth had stayed there that summer, but she didn't like it and wanted to come home so Mom let Martha go. She got her room and board and some pocket money for the chores she did, but she didn't have to do much. I envied her having a bedroom all to herself and getting all that good food that Aunt Lucy put on her table, particularly the tiny little pickles that she made from her garden and the homemade yeast bread that they had every day. I knew from Sunday School that it was wrong to envy, but I just couldn't help myself.

I was terribly excited whenever Mom let me go stay all night with Martha at Aunt Lucy's house. I guess Mom had talked with her, or Martha did, for every week or so, I was allowed to go. The day we talked to Mr. Cross about the wiener roast and the box supper was one of those lucky days.

I could hardly wait for the afternoon to pass, and as soon as it was over, we took off down the road west toward our church instead of going east to our house. For some strange reason, most of the people who lived in that direction were older and didn't have children in school so it was only Aunt Lucy's grandchildren that went that way. We walked with them until they turned off near the church then went on by ourselves.

"I hope she has some of the tiny pickles for supper," I said to Martha as we walked past the Guthrie farm. "Do you suppose she will?"

"I'm sure she will," answered Martha impatiently, "Since we have them every day."

"Don't you like them?"

"Of course, I like them, but you ask that same question every time you come over here."

"But I like them so much," I persisted. Then I asked Martha who I thought knew everything, "Why doesn't Mom make jars of little pickles instead of letting them get so big that she has to slice them up? Why doesn't she, Martha?"

And practical minded Martha knew the answer. "Because they go further that way, Ginny, and Mom always has to think about that with so many mouths to feed. Aunt Lucy doesn't have that problem."

I pondered that for awhile, then I asked, "Is that why Elizabeth is always saying that we are poor because we have so many mouths to feed?"

Martha stopped in the middle of the road and looked at me. "Yes, Ginny, that is one of the reasons. Another one is because Daddy was sick so long, but probably the main reason is that we are living in the Depression and most everybody is poor. Now, let's go before Aunt Lucy begins to worry about us." She started on and I slowly followed. I didn't really understand about the Depression, but I felt that Martha was in no mood for more questions now.

We walked a little while then I asked, "Reckon we'll have some of that delicious homemade yeast bread for supper?"

"I imagine so."

"I love it so much," I said.

This time Martha had to smile. "Do you come over here just for the food, Ginny?"

"I guess I do," I answered. Then I added quickly, "Oh, I like to be with you, and Aunt Lucy and Uncle Jake too, but the good food helps."

"Ginny, you're a mess," she said as we turned up the lane to the house.

"Do you suppose we'll get to listen to the radio?" I asked. This was another novelty since we didn't own one, not even the battery powered one.

"Probably, at least one program."

I breathed a sigh of deep contentment, and then turned my attention to the old garage on the left. Inside it, I knew that there was a big black car that hadn't been driven since Aunt Lucy's husband had died several years before. I didn't share this dream even with Martha, but ever since I had known about it, I had dreamed that since Aunt Lucy didn't drive that she would give it to us and then we'd have a car and could go anywhere in the world.

Now, I turned my attention to the long front porch where Aunt Lucy was standing to welcome us. She was a little woman with mousy gray hair, bright twinkly eyes covered with wire rimmed glasses, and she always wore a dress that reached almost to her ankles with a bib apron that almost covered the dress. I thought she was ancient, but I guess she was only in her sixties. Now, she smiled at me and said, "Hello, Ginny, glad that you could come." She seemed to like me and I certainly liked her. She patted my dark curls as I turned to speak to Uncle Jake.

He was seated in an old wooden rocker on the porch chewing his tobacco as he always did, and it dribbled down his chin as it always did. I wondered if his soft fried eggs that Aunt Lucy fixed him for breakfast would dribble down his chin as they usually did. He was old and fat and seldom said a word, but he smiled and nodded at me as I spoke to him.

Then Aunt Lucy was saying to Martha, "You'd best get changed so you can do your chores. You're later than usual."

Martha didn't answer, but just nodded as she signaled me with her eyes to follow her inside, and suddenly I knew why Elizabeth had not liked staying there for she didn't like for anyone to order her around, even Mom.

We left our lunch buckets in the kitchen and went to Martha's room where she changed to an old housedress that she wore for her chores. Since I was company, I didn't have to change. Her chores were gathering the eggs, sweeping the leaves off the walks and porches, and setting the table for supper. I knew that afterwards she would wash the dishes and sweep the kitchen. It wasn't much, but I guess Aunt Lucy thought she had to do something to earn her keep.

I helped her and particularly enjoyed setting the table for Aunt Lucy always had a white tablecloth on the long wooden table instead of the faded oilcloth that we had at home, and she kept her spoons in a glass container that I thought must be high priced crystal. And true to my expectations, we had the tiny pickles and the home made bread, and we also had fried canned sausage, canned green beans and fried potatoes with tall glasses of cold milk and even angel food cake for dessert.

We did get to listen to "Amos and Andy" on the radio after we finished the dishes and did our schoolwork at the kitchen table before we went to Martha's big bedroom that she had all to herself to put on our nightgowns for bed after that last trip out to the outdoor toilet.

Next morning at breakfast Uncle Jake did dribble the soft fried egg yolk down his chin, and I struggled to try to eat mine for I liked my eggs fried until they were "hard as a rock," as Daddy liked to tease me, and I couldn't stand the soft fried ones. But I gallantly ate them, too shy to tell her how I really liked them.

I helped Martha do the dishes while I watched Aunt Lucy pack our lunches with leftover cold sausage and bread, big red apples from her orchard, and pieces of the angel food cake. I knew it would be hard to concentrate on my work that morning as I anticipated that delicious lunch.

But I needn't have worried for Mr. Cross spent a lot of time that morning talking to the whole school about the box supper and the wiener roast, and we didn't have much time for lessons after all. We made plans to have the box supper the next week on a Friday night, and to have the wiener roast near the end of the month just before Halloween. I rushed home to share all of this good news with Mom and Daddy, walking to the mailbox with Ellen and Victor, and then running up the road north to our house. I missed walking with Martha, having her at home, and especially disliked having to do more and more of her work. It seemed that Elizabeth was always studying, or off wandering the fields, or hiding in the hayloft to write her poetry, and Janice was still too little to do much.

When Naomi came out to visit on Sunday afternoon, I hurried to greet her knowing that if I told her about our box supper, she'd find some way to send us some good things for our boxes. She was still working for Uncle Tobias and his mother who now lived with them. She got to come out about twice a week when they went to visit Vivian and Clifford.

I had got to go spend a whole week with her last summer, and I had had a glorious time. It was exciting to be in town that long, for they lived in a beautiful big house that had electricity, a basement where the furnace and washing machine were where Naomi did the washing and where I could play and read the stacks of colored funnies, and upstairs they even an indoor toilet and a big white bathtub. Naomi prepared delicious meals every day, and sometimes she took me downtown to buy me a bottle of orange Nehi, or a strawberry ice cream cone, or once to have my picture made at a real studio with my hair nicely curled and wearing a beautiful blue dress that she had bought me along with blue anklets, black leather shoes, and a big blue bow for my hair.

Now, I ran to her confident that she could supply my every wish. "Naomi," I said as I hugged her, "We're having a box supper at school next Friday night, and this will be my first one to go to. Could you get me some big red apples and some big red grapes like you did Elizabeth and Martha last year? Could you please?"

She laughed and hugged me again. "I'll see what I can do, Ginny," she promised as with me hanging on her arm, we made our way across the yard and into the house to see Mom. As always, she had brought Mom some little gift to make her work easier or lighter, and this time it was a new flour sifter that even had a handle to turn. Mom was delighted.

True to her word, Naomi sent out the apples and grapes by Uncle Tobias when he came out to Vivian's on Thursday night. She had gone to the movies with a friend.

Mom still had some young roosers that were tender enough to fry and she made a chocolate cake so with our fruit we had nice boxes which Elizabeth decorated with crepe paper and tied with fancy bows. Martha got to come home that night so she could go, and I hoped no one would talk about Aunt Lucy being alone in the house with Uncle Jake, but I didn't dare mention it for I wasn't supposed to know that was why Martha was there in the first place. I had just happened to overhear Mom talking to Daddy about it.

It was like the box suppers that Mom had told me about going to when she was young, and that Naomi, Elizabeth, and Martha had told me about in their turn. Chester Aston bought my box, and I was delighted to get to eat with the richest boy in school, but he hardly said a word and ate most of my good food. Mr. Cross did buy Elizabeth's box, and when she got the box of candy for being the prettiest girl, I figured that he'd paid a lot of the quarters for that too.

Now, Mr. Cross had the money to buy all the supplies for our big community wide wiener roast, and we all looked eagerly forward to that night. When the day finally arrived, he called off school that afternoon, (in those days, teachers could do that whenever they desired), and the whole school from the big seventh graders down to the smallest first graders trooped off to the woods to gather huge stacks of wood for the bonfire. We sounded like an army as we crashed through the woods, gathering brush, snapping sticks, and breaking limbs off dead trees. Mr. Cross and the bigger boys dragged back big pieces of wood to lay down first then we stacked the smaller ones higher and higher until it reached above our heads. Last, they stuffed little chips and pieces of wood down at the bottom to be used as kindling when they lighted the fire that night. I prayed that it wouldn't rain and spoil our fun even though the sky was blue and the clouds big, white, and fluffy like summer time. I thought I'd die if anything prevented us from having our wiener roast.

But God was good as usual, and the weather stayed nice. There was even a big full moon that night and it wasn't too cold. Mom and Daddy went to this event, hitching up the horses to the wagon so we could all ride, though Elizabeth thought it would be more dignified to walk. Martha was home again for the occasion, and even Joey, who was home for the weekend, went with us. I was so excited that I could hardly stand it. Daddy tied the team at one edge of the schoolyard where a couple of other wagons stood since most of the people had cars by then. Then we all hurried out back of where the pile of wood waited. Mom told us to watch Janice and Alice and went to help the other women with the food while Daddy wandered over to where the men were gathered by the basketball court talking crops and weather as they usually did. I took Alice's hand and led her over by the pile of wood for I wanted to be close when Mr. Cross lit the fire. I was so excited that I thought I would burst.

Finally, the great moment had arrived, and Mr. Cross came out to the woodpile carrying a big box of matches and followed by all the bigger boys and some of the smaller ones. I saw Burt following close to Victor, and Martha and Ellen came over with Janice holding Martha's hand rather unwillingly. Ginny was there with her sisters and brothers, but her mother had not come though most of the people in the community were there whether they had children or not.

Mr. Cross knelt near where I stood with little Alice, and I saw him open the box, take out a match and strike it. He held the blue flame close to the kindling, but it did not catch, and I realized that I had been holding my breath. But the second match caught and the flame grew bigger and bigger before our eyes as it caught the chips and little twigs then swept up the pile of smaller branches. Soon, the whole thing seemed to have caught fire and the sparks flew up into the sky as it crackled and glowed and burned. It was a glorious sight and one I would never forget.

GINNY'S DREAM

I felt a tap on my shoulder and looked up to see Martha's face in the darkness. She said to me in a voice filled with authority, "For goodness sakes, Ginny, get that baby away from the fire. Back up."

She had brought me back to reality and the magical moment was gone, but I was still excited. I gathered Alice up in my arms and ran with her up to where Mom sat on the recitation bench, that had been dragged from the schoolhouse, visiting with Milly, and practically threw Alice into her arms.

Then I ran back to the fire. The other kids played games of tag around the schoolhouse, or ran to play on the swings and teeter totter in the darkness, lit only by the full moon and glow from the fire, but I stood and watched the fire as it burned slower and slower, lower and lower, until only the big logs on the bottom were there, red hot with heat, and finally ready for roasting the wieners.

The men had sharpened long sticks torn from trees to put the wieners on, and they could roast several at a time. Daddy, Joey, and even Rex, who I think wanted to be my boy friend, offered to roast me one, but I wanted to do my own. I loved the feeling of piercing the hot dog through the middle with the stick then to hold it out to the fire, turning it over and over while my face and hands grew rosy from the heat, until it was roasted crusty brown, or what I called "just right." Then I'd cautiously pull it off, plop it into a bun, dab on the mustard, catsup, and relish and pop it into my mouth. Surely, nothing ever tasted so good! And the wonderful thing was that you could have all you wanted, and no one frowned, or shook their heads, or said, "Enough."

Skipping over Christmas, cold weather fun, and butchering that even Mr. Cross knew about, I'll tell about something else that we always did in Hickory Grove that he didn't know about. In late March, we girls decided that it was time to tell Mr. Cross what we usually did on the last day of school. We decided that Martha should be the spokesman, but Ellen, Ginny, and I trailed along. We sought out the teacher at his desk at lunch time as we had about the wiener roast in the fall. As we approached his desk, he looked up from the book he was reading and smiled.

"Yes, girls, what can I do for you?" he asked.

"Well, Mr. Cross," Martha began, "We thought that we should tell you about what we usually do on the last day of school."

"Oh, another tradition here at Hickory Grove?" he asked.

I pushed my way up closer to the desk. "What's a tradition?" I asked.

"That's something that you do over and over in almost the same way like the way you celebrate Christmas," he replied.

"Then this is a tradition," I told him, "For we've been doing it every year since I can remember."

"I guess I better find out what it is if it's that important." He smiled and closed his book.

Martha glared at me for taking over then smiled at the teacher as she explained. "The teacher rents a big stock truck, usually Emory Smith's, and we all ride in the back of the truck to Evansville, Indiana, where we go to the zoo and amusement park and—"

"And we have the most wonderful time," interrupted Ellen, "Oh, please say that we can go."

"You do still have some money from the box supper and the bake sale we had in January, don't you?"

"Yes, I have the money, but why do we need a big stock truck to take less than twenty-five people to Evansville?"

"Oh, everyone goes," I broke in. "All the mothers and some of the fathers and the little ones at home, and they bring big baskets of food for our shared dinner in the park."

"Do the high schoolers go too?" he asked.

"Yes, some of them do and I'm sure that Elizabeth will go if you ask her," I answered while Martha glared at me again. But he just smiled, leaned back in his chair and clasped his hands together.

"Sounds like a good idea to me," he finally said, "I'll get in touch with this Emory Smith right away to see if we can use his truck."

So, for the last month of school we had this exciting trip to Evansville to look forward to, the farest place that most of us had ever been except Chester Aston who had been all the way out west.

GINNY'S DREAM

Despite all my prayers to the contrary, when I woke up on the last day of school, it was raining, not hard but a good slow drizzle.

"Now, we won't get to go," were the first words out of Martha's mouth when she looked out the window.

"Oh, we have to. We just have to," I protested jumping out of bed and running to the window to press my forehead against the cool glass.

Even Elizabeth was cross for she had made plans to miss high school so she could go and she certainly didn't want to waste a day if we had to just stay at the school and have our lunch there.

Only Mom was calm as usual. "Perhaps it'll clear up before it's time to go," she told us. "Quit being so unhappy."

But it continued to rain while we dressed and had breakfast, and was still drizzling when Daddy went to hitch the team to the wagon to take us to school for Mom and the little girls were going too. It had stopped by the time we reached the school, but the sky was still overcast and it looked like it might pour any minute.

My hopes were dashed when we went inside for some of the parents who didn't want to get wet in the back of the truck for it had high sides but no top, were trying to persuade the teacher to just stay there, have our dinner and play some games. All of us kids wanted to go despite the rain and begged to do that. Poor Mr. Cross didn't know what to do.

Then Randall and Sarah came in with their basket of food and he said to all of us, "It's all right. The sun is going to shine. I even saw a bit of blue sky when we came in. I say, 'Let's go!'" I don't know whether or not it was because Randall was a leader in our church and our community, or what but the others trusted him and we went. And it didn't rain. By the time we got to Evansville, about forty miles away, the sun was shining.

What a wonderful day it was! It was fun riding in the back of the truck sitting on old rugs or quilts, laughing, singing, and telling jokes. They put chairs in for the women and a couple of grandmas rode up in the cab with Emory. When we got there, we were divided up into small groups to go with some adult supervisors to the zoo. I was happy that I got to go with Mr. Cross and Elizabeth, and I didn't laugh when I caught them holding hands.

By the time we got back from the zoo, the mothers who didn't go had several tables covered with long white cloths and the baskets of food set out. Since I loved to eat, this was a part that I loved. There was so much good food that it was hard to choose. I tried three kinds of pie and had a piece of chocolate cake plus all the ham, fried chicken, and vegetables that I ate.

After we rested awhile, the teacher and some of the adults took us over to the amusement park where we happily spent our tightly clutched dimes and nickels riding the Ferris wheel, the merry-go-round, the tilt a whirl, and swings that went round and round faster and faster, higher and higher. I liked the merry-go-round the best and rode it twice. It was fun just to watch the rides when our money ran out.

Back at the picnic tables we ate again then played on the slides and swings that were nearby. We were almost ready to go home when Janice ran over to the swings and got too close. Before Rex could stop his swing, he had hit her in the head and knocked her down. He jumped out and ran to her yelling, "Come quick. I've knocked Janice down."

We all ran, but I think Mom got there first. She knelt on the grass cradling Janice's blonde braids in her arms. Janice's eyes were closed and there was a knot on her head as big as a goose egg.

I thought, "Oh, my goodness, she's dead, and it's my fault for insisting that we come despite the rain."

But one of the kids was eating a snowcone and the teacher snatched it from him, dumped the ice in his handkerchief, and handed it to Mom to put on the bump. Pretty soon Janice opened her eyes, looked around and started to cry. Mom held the ice on until it all melted and the water ran down her fingers, and by that time the swelling had mostly gone down. They decided that it was safe to move her so we gathered up all our things and trooped back to the truck.

On the way home, I leaned back against Ginny's shoulder, tired and happy. "I'm sure glad that we have such nice traditions at Hickory Grove," I thought to myself as the big truck rumbled down the highway towards home.

Now, back to Christmas, cold weather fun, and butchering.

Chapter 7

Butchering

M uch to our disappointment, it didn't snow for that Christmas. We had a lovely Christmas anyway, but it was always more exciting when it snowed. Now, that I no longer believed in Santa Claus I didn't have to worry how he would get down the chimney since we had a heating stove with a long pipe attached to the flue. When I was little, I used to beg Mom to let the fire go out on Christmas Eve so he wouldn't get burnt, but when it turned out to be a bitter cold day, I was glad that she hadn't. Naomi and Joey both got to come home from their jobs on Christmas Eve, and we were all glad to see them plus happy over the fruit, nuts, candy, and small gifts that they brought us. I enjoyed helping fix Janice and Alice's stockings and even one for myself because Naomi insisted.

But the next week during our vacation from school, it snowed and snowed and snowed. I knew it made doing the chores and caring for the livestock more difficult for I often helped Daddy when Elizabeth was gone, or busy doing something else. We had to shovel paths to the barn and woodpile and well before we could begin to do the work, and by the time we came back to the back porch with full arms of chopped firewood, buckets of water or warm foamy milk, we had to stomp our feet and brush off our coats with a broom before we were allowed in the kitchen. But the snow was so beautiful and so much fun to play in! It was as though fairyland had come to our part of the country overnight.

The first morning when I awoke in our cold bedroom and looked out the window, I leaped out of bed with a cry of joy that quickly turned to one of pain for the linoleum was so cold to my bare feet that I thought I'd die. I jumped back up on the bed and began tugging at Martha who was still snuggled down under the heavy pile of covers.

"Martha, wake up. It snowed. Oh, do wake up and see how pretty it is." I kept on tugging until Martha opened her eyes and looked at me in a grumpy way.

"For goodness sakes, Ginny, can't you let a body sleep? I'll be wishing I had stayed at Aunt Lucy's instead of coming home for vacation." She shut her eyes and turned over pulling the covers up to her nose.

I always wondered why Aunt Lucy and Uncle Jake could stay alone during vacations but not during school weeks, but I never bothered to ask anyone.

"But the snow is so pretty and I'm so excited about it." I crawled back under the covers but still sat up so I could look out the window.

Just then five year old Janice, who had been asleep on the other side of Martha, sat up and said in her bright cheerful voice, "I'll be excited with you, Ginny. I like the snow." Then as she looked out the window, she cried, "Oh, how pretty!"

"Good for you, Janice. We'll go play in it and just let grumpy old Martha sleep." I jumped out of bed again, ran quickly to the other side of the bed, grabbed Janice up in my arms and ran for the front room where I knew there would be a warm fire.

By the time we'd had our breakfast and I'd helped Daddy with the chores, Martha was up and about, her usual cheerful self, busy as always, feeding Alice, washing the dishes in a dishpan on the back of the kitchen range, then sweeping the kitchen floor. So, when Janice and I started putting on our long pants, coats, hats, gloves, and pulling overshoes on over our shoes, she was ready to join us for a frolic in the snow.

It was delightful outside as it wasn't terribly cold, and it was still snowing. We tramped through it for awhile, making snowballs, and running with the dogs. Then I suggested, "Let's go down to Ellen's and go down the big hill on their sled. Want to, Martha?"

"Sure, that sounds like fun. Go ask Mom if it's ok."

"I want to go too," put in Janice who was scrambling up from the ground where Shep had knocked her over in his exuberance of play. "I want to go too."

"Yes, Janice, you can go," surprisingly it was me and not tender hearted Martha who was giving in. I guess I was remembering her shared excitement earlier in bed.

Mom gave her permission with a reminder to be careful and to watch out for Janice, and we were off down the lane to Ellen's house. She, Victor, and Bert were already outside sliding down the big hill in front of their house on a long sled that their dad had made. They greeted us with cries of welcome and quickly we joined their fun. Martha and Ellen took the little ones with them so I ended up riding with Victor. I put my arms around his waist and held on tightly, dreadfully afraid, but unwilling to not go for the excitement far outmeasured the fear. There were several spills, but no one was hurt, and we were only wet and cold when Milly called us to come inside to dry off and have some hot chocolate.

It stopped snowing, but it continued to get colder, and it was only a couple of days later that Daddy announced after he came back from Clifford's one morning that the pond was frozen and that we could go skating on it safely.

"Only if you go along with them," said Mom with sudden authority. "There's always the chance that one of you might break through the ice so you go with them, Joe."

"Good, I love to go skating," I shouted as I ran for my wraps and overshoes. We never had skates, or even knew that we should have had skates. We just slid around on the ice and thought that it was a wonderful sport.

"Let's take the tub too. It's such fun to glide across the ice in the tub," said Elizabeth who had decided to go with us.

"I'll get the tub," volunteered Martha as she pulled on her overshoes.

But when Janice began to put on her things, it was Mom who decided that she was too little, that it was too cold, and that she would stay home with her and little Alice, and it was Mom who listened to her screams when we left.

What fun we had! We glided and twirled across the ice as though we were ladies of the king's court. Daddy didn't skate with us though Elizabeth said that he used to when she was little. He leaned on the railfence that surrounded the pond and watched us while we skated, holding hands or on our own. But he did shove us across the ice as one by one we climbed in the tub, held on tightly and practically swooped across the pond. We had such a good time I wished that it would never end, but, of course, it did, and we had to go home to do the chores, and help Mom with supper. Janice had stopped crying and was happily playing paper dolls behind the heating stove while Alice tried to take them everytime she turned her head. Such were the joys of a big family!

Next day it was somewhat warmer so we took both the little girls out with us while we built a huge snowman in the front yard. Joey was home that day and he helped us roll the big big ball for the body. It was a good thing for it was so heavy that we couldn't have moved it. Then we rolled a smaller one for the chest and a little one for the head.

"Let's put a hat on the snowman," suggested Janice as she patted its cold firm body.

"Hat, snowman, hat, snowman," repeated little Alice looking up at us with her brown eyes while her red curls straggled out of her tied on cap.

"Sure, why not?" agreed Elizabeth. "I'll go get a hat and a scarf for his neck," as she ran for the back porch.

"Wait a minute and I'll get something else for him," said Joey as he went out behind the smokehouse where we dumped the ashes from the stoves. Soon he was back carrying pieces of black burnt wood which he carefully placed on the snowman's head for eyes, nose, mouth, and ears.

Then Elizabeth was back with an old hat and scarf which she put on his head and around his neck. It was a glorious snowman we all agreed. But I thought he needed one thing more and I went to the back porch for our old broom. Most of the bristles were gone, but it was perfect for what I wanted. "This can be the arms," I said holding out the broom to Joey.

"I believe you're right, Ginny," he said taking the broom and thrusting the handle straight through the middle ball so that it looked like arms even if one side did have bristles on it.

I went to the kitchen window and pounded on it. "Mom, Daddy, come see our wonderful snowman," I called. And out they came pulling their coats and hats on as they came, and with Mom getting her shoes wet in the snow. It was a happy moment for all of us standing there in the snow looking at our creation—the grandest snowman of all time.

That night after supper we had another advantage of the snow. Mom took her dishpan out in the orchard where the snow was still white and clean and dipped up a whole dishpan full. Then back in the kitchen she added some sugar, vanilla, and thick cream that she dipped off a crock of milk that was setting on the long table to it, mixed it up, dished it out in bowls and we all enjoyed delicious snow ice cream. I really loved it when it snowed!

The next few days it got colder and colder. No matter how many covers we piled on the beds, we could never get really warm. The milk froze in crocks in the kitchen and the water in the water bucket. It was hard to drag ourselves out of bed, get the chores done, and walk to school in that unbelievable cold weather. We didn't wear pants to school back then, and our long brown cotton stockings just came to our knees. By the time we got to school, our legs above our knees would be bright red and so cold we could hardly move. Everyone stayed in at recesses and played marbles or checkers, or games on the blackboards.

One thing that I always liked about really cold weather was that was when we had Butchering Day. Sure enough just the next week Daddy announced one night at supper, "I've decided that it's cold enough to butcher without the meat spoiling so I've decided to do it on Friday. I talked to Clifford and Albert today, and they'll tell Enos and

Randell. Friday is all right with you, isn't it, Pauline?" he asked my mother as she brought a big dish of navy beans and another of fried potatoes to the table while I carried the plate of hot cornbread.

My mother laughed as she sat down. "I guess it is, Joe, since you've already decided," then when he started to protest, she added, "No, really, it's fine. It'll be good to have fresh meat on our table again." It was a common joke around our house that we had beans and potatoes one day and potatoes and beans the next except in summer when we had vegetables from the garden and chickens from the henhouse, and when we butchered in the winter.

As we ate supper, we made plans for the Butchering Day, and I asked as I always did something that I never asked any other time, and that was to be allowed to stay home from school that day. It was such an exciting day and I didn't want to miss a single minute of it. Much to the surprise of everyone knowing how much value Mom put on school, she agreed and I was elated.

I could hardly wait until Friday, and when I went to bed on Thursday night, I reminded my mother, "Be sure and call me before anything happens."

Nevertheless I was surprised when she woke me by gently shaking my shoulder and whispering so she wouldn't wake up the little girls, or Elizabeth as it wasn't time for her to get up for school yet. "Ginny, it's time to get up. It's Butchering Day."

I opened my eyes and looked around. It was still pitch black dark and it was very cold in our bedroom. But

I could see that Mom was fully dressed, and she reminded me as she turned away. "You said that you didn't want to miss anything. Bring your clothes in by the fire to get dressed."

"But why is it so dark?" I asked.

"Because it is very early."

"Why do we have to start so early?"

"Because there is so much to do. Are you coming or not?" She went back into the front room and closed the door.

"Sure, I'm coming," I called. Then remembering the little ones and Elizabeth still asleep, I bravely jumped out of the warm bed, grabbed up my clothes and ran for the fire. "Wow! It's cold!" I edged close to the stove and held out my hands.

She laughed as she added some big chunks of wood to the glowing fire in the stove. "Sure you don't want to sleep later and go on to school?"

"No, I'm sure I want to stay here and help."

"Then dress very warmly. Here's an extra sweater I dug out." She handed me the sweater and headed for the kitchen.

"Where's Daddy?"

She turned at the door before going through their cold bedroom on the way to the kitchen. "He's already doing the chores. Are you helping him or me?"

"Him," I answered. "I want to tell the sows goodby."

She nodded and went out shutting the door. I took off my nightgown and quickly dressed in the warmest clothes I had even adding the extra sweater. Except for what Naomi bought me for good, or Mom made, all of my clothes were hand me downs from the older girls, or clothes that some well meaning neighbor or relative had given us. I hated most of them.

Mom was making pie dough when I went through the kitchen, but I saw the big pan of oatmeal simmering on the stove, and smelled biscuits baking in the oven. Tomorrow, there will be fresh meat, I thought to myself as I pulled on my overshoes and outer wraps, opened the kitchen door and went out into the cold darkness. The stars were still shining and it looked like nighttime. I shivered as I went off the porch and down the path toward the barn. The dogs, asleep on old rugs in the corner of the porch where it was warmer, lifted their heads and looked at me, but didn't get up.

I thought about the sows that were going to die so we could have fresh meat, smoked hams and bacon and lard by the canful. It made me sad for I hated for anything to have to die, but being a farm girl, I knew that pigs and chickens and sometimes cows, though we didn't raise that kind, had to die to provide food, and I did love to eat. One summer I had made one of the baby chickens my pet and taught it to follow me and always fed it special. I had named it George, and when it turned out to be a hen, it was still George. I had begged Mom not to kill her, and it was still there though she didn't lay many eggs anymore. I always hid my head, or ran inside when Daddy wrung the young roosters' heads off in the summertime so we could have fried chicken, or the old hens' heads in the winter so we could have chicken and dumplings. And when Mom chopped their heads off with an axe and made me hold their legs, I shut my eyes and turned my head. I wondered how they did it.

Inside the barn, I went first to the big stable where the two huge sows had been penned up. The other pigs were out in the pighouse so they wouldn't be hurt when the guns were fired. I knew that I would be back in the house by then and would hold my hands tightly over my ears when the shots were fired. Now, I peeped through the crack and saw them eating. Daddy was tender hearted like me so I guess he had given them a good last breakfast.

"Goodby," I called softly through the cracks. "I'm sorry that you have to die, but we really need all the good food that you're going to give us. Thank you."

Hearing movement behind me in the entry way, I turned quickly and saw Daddy bringing Jersey out of her stall and carrying the milk bucket. "Hi, Punken," he said calling me by the nickname he often used. "So, you did get up early to help. How about milking Jersey for me while I finish the feeding? Then we need to get the fire going in the pit."

"Okay." I took the bucket and squatted on the ground beside gentle old Jersey. I had to take off my gloves so I could squeeze and pull her teats for the milk to come and my hands nearly froze. But I leaned my head against Jersey's flank and she felt warm. The milk first pinged in the bucket then as it got fuller it steadily sloshed until finally I was through. It seemed weird milking in the dark this way. Then Daddy had me put her back in the stall as it was still too dark and cold to put her out to pasture. I carried one of the big buckets of milk as we went back to the house.

When we entered the kitchen, glad for the warmth of the fire, Elizabeth was up and dressed, standing by the stove stirring a pan of custard and raisins for the baked pie shells on the end of the long table. Mom was pouring canned blackberries into unbaked shells to prepare them for the oven. Elizabeth looked at me with a wicked grin.

"Well, so you are playing hooky today?"

I set the milk bucket on the table and began to pull off my overshoes and wraps. "Not really," I answered. "Mom said that I could stay home to help. It's such an exciting day! Are you staying home too, Elizabeth?"

"No way. I'd much rather go to school." She lifted the pan from the stove and began to pour it into the pans. I could hardly wait until dinnertime for that was my favorite kind of pie.

Daddy had removed his wraps and sat down at the table. One thing about my daddy he expected to be waited on, and my mom had been doing it for years. Since I was helping today, I filled his bowl with hot oatmeal, his cup with hot coffee from the big pot on the back of the stove, handed him some biscuits, butter, and applebutter, and then got my own. Elizabeth soon joined us, but Mom just kept on working. I often wondered if she didn't get awful tired sometimes. She was only thirty-nine, but seemed much older.

When we had finished eating, Daddy and I put back on our outdoor things, and went back out in the darkness.

We went back behind the smokehouse and around to the side of the yard next to the orchard. Here Daddy and Joey had dug a deep pit and had put firewood down in it. On top of the firewood was a big long black iron kettle that he had borrowed from Uncle Albert. It was full of water that we had carried from the cistern last night. Now, I stood filled with excitement while Daddy knelt and struck matches to light the fire. I knew that it would heat the water until it was scalding hot, and I knew that they would dip the sows in that water after they were dead and before they hung them up on the iron hooks that were attached to the tall maple tree so they could scrape them.

"We won't do anymore until the water boils so you might as well go inside out of the cold for awhile," my father said as he stood up and put his arm around me. I think he knew that I would stay inside until after the pigs were dead. So I turned and ran back inside the house.

It was just turning daylight and I had already washed the dishes and made the beds when the first neighbors arrived. My cousin Vivian and her husband Clifford came first as they just lived down the road. She was about twenty years older than me and always seemed more like a big sister than a cousin. They lived in my uncle's old house where my mother and father had been married on Christmas Day twenty years ago. She came in the back door taking off her wraps with a cheerful good morning for all of us. She wore a clean print dress which she had made and a bib apron that nearly covered the dress.

"Well, are you girls staying home to help?" she asked as she bent over to undo her overshoes.

GINNY'S DREAM

"I am," I answered quickly. "I think this is such an exciting day."

"I'm not," said Elizabeth who was peeling mounds of potatoes at the little table. "And I really need to go get ready for school, Mom."

"Then run along and I'll peel potatoes," said Vivian moving to the table and taking over the job. She had brought two apple pies to add to the feast.

Just then the shots rang out and I hadn't even had time to cover my ears. I looked at Mom in dismay, but she just said, "Better get your things on if you're going to go watch, Ginny. I'll need you later to get Alice dressed and fix her and Janice's breakfast. But run along now."

Bundled up again I ran outside where the sky was just turning red in the east. Down at the barn, they were dragging the dead hogs out of the barn by hooks that they had attached to their feet. Uncle Albert and Enos were there too, and I knew by the big knife that Uncle Albert held in his hand that he had been the one to slit their throats so they would bleed after they were shot. He always teased us girls and called us boys, and none of us were too fond of him. Even now, he looked at me and said, "What do we have here? The boy has come to help us."

I didn't answer, but followed as they dragged the sows up past the house to where the roaring fire had the water boiling. By this time Randall and Sarah, Mom's cousin, who lived down the road from the school, were there, and she had gone inside to help carrying with her two big loaves of her homemade yeast bread. I could hardly wait until dinnertime.

I watched as they lifted the heavy hogs, struggling with their dead weight, and dropped them in the water. This was to soften them up so they could scrape off the skin. Then they lifted them out and hung them up on the strong hooks attached to the trees. Next they took blunt edged knives and began to scrape off the skin.

"Here, boy, you can help too," and Uncle Albert handed me a piece of broken glass which I used to scrape down low where I could reach. It all seemed exciting and I felt grown up and important.

When this job was finished, they split the undersides from throat to hind legs and all the guts and icky stuff poured out. This part I really didn't like so I went back inside because I knew they had to wait now for the meat to cool before they spread it out on the sawhorse table and cut up the hams, shoulders, sides of bacon, and liver. They built up the fire to keep warm and stood around talking. I spent the rest of the morning going outside to watch, and inside to help.

Just before time for the noontime meal, Daddy brought in a big pan of tenderloin and liver for Mom to fry. I felt jealous that we were going to have to share this delicious fresh meat with these people, and I knew that Mom would give them more of it when they left to go home. It made me angry for I knew they all had more than we did, and I felt that we shouldn't have to share. But when I had complained to Mom about this last year, she had tried to explain that we couldn't use all the fresh meat quickly enough and that it would spoil, and she'd also reminded me not to be so selfish.

It was the custom in those days for the men to always eat first so I had to wait impatiently until they had eaten and eaten, until I wondered if there would be anything left, before I could eat. But it was worth waiting for. How delicious that food was!

In the afternoon, they dipped the big shoulders and hams into barrels of heavy salt water to help to preserve them. Then they hung them from rafters in the smokehouse and built a fire of hickory wood in the little stove in there so that it would just smoke and further preserve the meat plus give it the wonderful hickory flavor.

They also took all the fat from the hogs, cut it up in little pieces, boiled it in a huge round iron kettle over the fire until it was clear then after it was cool, they ran it through a lard press and into large cans — pure white lard that would be stored for use in frying and baking for as long as it lasted. We didn't know about the dangers of cholesterol in those days.

The women gathered up scraps of the meat, seasoned it with salt, pepper, and sage and ran it through a grinder making sausage that they stored in the cleaned out intestines of the hogs. Later Mom would fry it all up and pack it in jars that were sealed tightly so it would stay good a long time. They even cut up and cooked parts of the heads and feet making a jellied loaf called headcheese — a dish that I did not ever like.

When I went to bed that night, my parents, who had been up so early in the morning, were still working taking care of the fresh meat. I knew they were proud that they had so much good food for our family.

As I said my prayers, in bed because it was too cold to kneel on the floor, I thanked God for all the delicious meat, and then I asked Him to forgive me for being so selfish about serving it to the ones who had helped and particularly for the way I felt about them taking it home with them. But somehow to me it never seemed right. Nevertheless, it had been an exciting and busy day, and I was so tired I couldn't go to sleep for a very long time.

Chapter 8

Cattle Drive

The highlight of that spring was that I was considered old enough to be in the county track meet. I got to run the fifty yard dash. I didn't win, but I did come in second and that red ribbon was mighty precious in my eyes. I hung it up over the dresser in the bedroom so I could see it the first thing when I opened my eyes each morning.

After that, school was soon out and we were all busy planting the big garden down by the barn, and the huge potato patch that seemed to stretch to eternity when we had to hoe it later. Martha was back home for good as she wanted to come home and Mom needed her. We were all glad to have her back, me particularly for I had been doing much of her work.

GINNY'S DREAM

Mom always ordered baby chickens from the hatchery, and they sent them by mail in a big box with tiny holes in the top so they could breathe. Our mailman always brought them right up to the house for he couldn't very well leave those baby chicks outside the mailbox and they wouldn't fit inside. When we saw his old car puffing up the lane, we knew that this was the day. How exciting it was to open the lid and see those hundred, actually it was one hundred two in case some died along the way, tiny yellow baby chicks with all of them saying, "Peep, peep" at the same time!

That summer I often went through the field west of our house where the big ditches were and on up the path to the little three room cabin where the Bates family lived. There was an elderly couple and his brother who was hard of hearing that lived there. Their house had never been painted and it was blackened from the weather. There was a long front porch, with a front room and bedroom across the front and kitchen at the back. They had a high topped chest in the front room that I thought was beautiful. Mr. Bates played the fiddle when I begged him real hard and I thought that was beautiful too. They always seemed glad to see me and she usually had a big pan of hot cornbread with freshly churned butter to spread on it, and she always gave me some. I thought it was strange that she kept her suitcase packed and under her bed in case her son-in-law had a heart attack in the middle of the night and she had to go. The stranger thing was that he lived much longer than she did.

GINNY'S DREAM

One of the reasons that I liked to go there was because she told me stories. She was the seventh daughter of a seventh daughter and she could cure nosebleeds and all sorts of ills. A long time ago there was a cemetery under the big cedar trees in front of their house, and she told me stories about how on moonlit nights the spirits would rise out of the graves and walk through the fields. I would get so scared that there would be prickles on the back of my neck, but I always went back for more.

On other early summer mornings, I was sent out with a big bucket to that same field to pick dewberries that grew on briars right on the ground. I would sit on the ground, pick the berries, which were big and round and oh, so juicy and good, putting some in the bucket and some in my mouth. It took me a long time to fill a bucket, but I had a delightful time lost in my world of make believe and dreams. When I finally got home dragging the heavy bucket behind me, Mom would take some off the top to wash and "sugar down" for dinner. If they were good in the field, they were even better with a thick coating of sugar.

On one such pleasant summer afternoon when the sky was blue with big fluffy clouds that resembled all sorts of creatures and the shade from the big maples in our front yard was a good place to study them, I lay on my back in the thick grass and stared upward. Suddenly, I realized that someone was there, and looking up, I saw Ellen, Victor, and Burt staring down at me.

"Hello," said Ellen. "What on earth are you doing?"

I rolled over and sat up. "Nothing except looking at the clouds. I like to figure out different shapes that I see in them."

"Oh, Ginny, you are weird," said Victor as he sat down on the grass beside me.

"I am not," I retorted. Then turning to Ellen who had flopped down beside me. "What's up? What do you want to do?"

"We thought maybe we could go down to the creek to play," she said. "Where is Martha?" Ellen was glad too that Martha was no longer staying at Aunt Lucy's for they were best of friends and had always been.

"She's helping Mom can berries."

"Why aren't you helping too?" teased Victor.

"Because I picked most of the berries, and besides I'm too little to can," I spat back. Victor and I were really very good friends, but most of the time picked on one another. "Come on. Let's go see if she's about through."

We jumped up and ran for the back porch while Burt joined Janice who was playing with little cars in the dirt by the flower beds. The kitchen was hot from the heat of the range where a kettle of berries were simmering. Mom, as usual was barefoot, and she looked hot and tired. But her smile was warm as she greeted our friends. Martha was washing half gallon jars in a pan of hot soapy dishwater.

"Are you about through, Martha?" I asked. "We want to go to the creek to play."

She poured boiling water from the teakettle into the jars in another dishpan and then looked at Mom.

"Sure," Mom said. "Run along. This is the last batch and I can manage by myself. Alice is asleep and you can take Janice with you." She smiled again and turned back to her work.

Martha dried her hands and we hurried out the back door, went around the house to collect the little ones, and were soon walking down the path to the creek. The grass in the pasture was still green from the spring rains and wild flowers were blooming. It was a good time to be young and alive.

At the creek, we sat down to rest; then decided to go wading in the cold water which we did from our fence all the way up to the bridge. Then we climbed the bluff until we reached the spring where sparkling cold water gushed out. We took turns kneeling and drinking from our hands with Martha and Ellen, as usual, helping Janice and Burt to get a drink. After a game of tag, using certain trees for our safe bases, we fell to the ground under the shade of an old oak tree to rest and visit.

After a moment of silence, I suggested, "Let's ask our mothers if we can camp out back here tomorrow night."

"You mean stay all night?" questioned Ellen.

"Sure, why not?"

"Because you'd be scared and keep us awake all night for one thing," said Victor.

"I would not be," I argued.

"What about old man Jones?" asked Ellen in a scary voice, and we all laughed. Many years ago when my father was a young man, some men were drinking and they got into a fight. One of the men killed another one with a knife then they brought him to this bluff and hanged him on a small tree. Since then everyone had called it Jones's Bluff, and no one ever wanted to walk up the hill past the creek at nighttime for fear of his ghost.

"That's nonsense," said practical minded Martha. "We know there is no such thing as ghosts or spirits despite what Mrs. Bates says," as she looked at me. "And besides, we don't have to sleep here. We can go to the other bluff over by Clifford's. I think it might be fun."

When Martha liked an idea, it seemed almost settled so we all nodded our heads. As usual, Burt and Janice were off by themselves digging in a pile of dirt with some sticks, making tunnels and whatnot. Now, Ellen nodded in their direction, and said in a low voice, "Let's don't bring them," and we all agreed.

Our mothers readily gave their consent, and our plans were made. We took old blankets for our beds, and raided our kitchens for our food. Much to my delight, Ellen brought peanut butter and crackers, fried apple pies which Milly made, and a jar of grape Kool-Aid for our supper. We took boiled potatoes and eggs, fresh lettuce and radishes from our garden, and Mom's homemade chocolate drop cookies. For our breakfast, we all took eggs, some cured bacon, cold biscuits, and a big jar of milk. We planned to build a fire and had a skillet to cook the eggs and bacon in. The milk, eggs and bacon were put in a bucket wrapped in an old towel to put in the creek to keep them fresh. Our leaving was joyous except for Janice's sobbing that she wanted to go too.

We felt full of adventure and excitement as we hurried along the path toward the bluff. The sun was low in the west and we all knew that soon it would be gone and then it would be dark. We'd all slept out in the yard on hot summer nights, and Ellen and Victor had sometimes slept down at the river with their dad when he went fishing, but never had we slept out over night by ourselves on the bluff, particularly with Jones's Bluff and its curse so nearby.

First we set up camp, choosing the trees where we would fix our beds and gathering wood for our breakfast fire. Martha took our things to the creek where she carefully lodged the bucket between two big logs. Then we chose trees in one direction for the girls' toilet and in the other direction for the boys though we had only Victor. Leaving our supper near our beds, we played games—Stink Base, Hoopey Hide, May I?, and Tag—until we were exhausted. We noticed that the sun had almost set by the time we went down to the creek to wash our faces and hands before we ate our supper which we spread out on our bed blankets careful not to spill the Kool-Aid.

"This is what I call living," I said as I bit into one of Milly's delicious fried apple pies. "Why don't we do this more often?"

"It's not dark yet," said Victor.

"What's that got to do with anything?" I asked.

"Well, the ghosts haven't started coming through the trees," he said in a low threatening voice.

"Oh, Victor, do be quiet," scolded Ellen, and Martha frowned at him.

As the twilight slowly turned to darkness, we sat close together on one of the blankets telling stories and singing songs, all of us a little afraid, but not willing to admit it. After a long time, we went to our toilets in the bushes and then fully dressed rolled up in our blankets and tried to go to sleep.

"Just say your prayers to yourself," whispered Martha, and I tried, but all that came to my mind was, "Dear God, don't let there be any ghosts or spirits tonight." Then I added quickly, "I don't believe in them anyway." But I still couldn't go to sleep. I think it was a very long time before any of us slept.

But we were all asleep when I awoke with a start. I had heard a sound that awoke me. I opened my eyes cautiously and peered into the darkness, and when I saw the two huge shapes, my heart leaped to my throat I was that scared. I inched closer to Martha poking her back while I whispered hoarsely, "Martha, wake up. Wake up for goodness sakes."

Martha stretched and yawned and tried to move away from my probing fingers, but I wouldn't let her. "Oh, Ginny, go back to sleep," she said crossly.

"But Martha, there's something here. They're big and dark and scary."

At my words, Victor woke up and seeing the dark shapes, practically threw himself into Ellen's arms for she was now awake and sitting up. Martha and I sat up too with my arm entwined in hers and we all sat there with our hearts pounding. It's one thing to say you don't believe in spirits and it's another to see an unknown thing on a dark night near Jones's Bluff.

Suddenly, Martha began to laugh and we all looked at her like she had suddenly gone crazy. But just then the moon came out from behind a cloud, and we all saw why she was laughing. Our fearsome spirits were only Old Jersey and Susie, our friendly cows, having a midnight snack. Daddy had turned them out to pasture instead of leaving them in the barnlot as he usually did.

"Well, who's afraid of spirits now?" I laughed at Victor who still clung to his older sister.

"You were scared too," he challenged.

But I denied it knowing that I was lying as I did. "Oh, no, I knew it was the cows all the time."

It was nearly daylight before we slept again, and then we woke when the sun began to get hot. Victor started the fire while Ellen and I went to the creek for our breakfast. But there we had a big disappointment. Some creatures, probably raccoons, had tipped over the bucket, broken the eggs and eaten the raw bacon while the water had not been cool enough to keep our milk from souring. So, we picked some wild blackberries growing nearby and ate them with some cookies left from the night before as we gathered around the fire as though we were real pioneers. We had survived our first real camping trip and met the challenges.

One of my favorite things that summer was going to spend a few days, or maybe even a whole week with my mother's sister, Aunt Marie and Uncle Leonard. They didn't have any children, and I thought they were rich for they had so many things, even electricity. I liked to pretend that I was theirs and could have anything I wanted, even a bicycle, but after I had been there a few days, I began to get homesick for Mom and Daddy, and even my sisters, and was glad to come home. They had a shady grape arbor where I liked to read or daydream, and I ate so many grapes that's it's a wonder I didn't die of stomach-ache. I liked to sit on top of the rail fence that surrounded their barnlot and watch them milk their cows, and sometimes they let me help. We ate bologna, canned potted meat, store bought cookies, and had Kool-Aid and strawberry jello almost every day. Sometimes, I sneaked into her bedroom and chewed her already chewed gum that she'd left on a little dish on her dresser. Then I'd put it back and vow that someday I'd have fresh chewing gum every day.

Uncle Leonard liked to tease me, but I loved him and didn't mind. He had a car and I loved the places that he took me. He told me once that he was going to take me to Twinway where we would see streetcars. I had read about them in a book that they had given me so I was excited about seeing the real thing. When we arrived in Twinway, it was a tiny little town, and there were certainly no streetcars.

"Where are they?" I cried.

He laughed and ruffled my curls. "Right there," and he pointed to some cars moving down the street. "Those are cars in the street."

Another time he promised me mountains, and I believed him even though I knew there were no mountains in southern Illinois. They turned out to be banks of clouds at sunset.

He was a horse trader besides being a farmer, and many a long hour I sat in the car with Aunt Marie waiting for him to make a deal. One day I vowed to her, "I'll never marry a horse trader and you can bet on that." She just laughed and I thought she was a very patient lady.

It was late that summer when my Uncle Albert came down one night to ask Mom if Martha and me could help him drive his cattle from his farm up to another farm he owned north of Carmon which was about ten miles. He said that his daughter would drive the car so we could ride part of the way, but he needed help getting them across highways and creeks. He promised to pay us which made it seem more intriguing to us, and when Mom looked to us for approval, we both nodded our heads.

"Good," he said. "See you in the morning at seven o'clock," then he added the hated word, "boys." As he was getting in his car, he called back, "Better bring some lunch as it'll take all day."

"How much money do you think he will give us?" I asked Martha as we got ready for bed.

"Oh, probably a dollar apiece," she answered.

"Maybe even two dollars apiece," I mused as I climbed into bed.

"Ginny, you're such a dreamer," Martha answered as she settled in beside me.

Mom woke us early the next morning, and by the time we were dressed, she had breakfast ready and a lunch packed in a paper bag that we could throw away.

"Better wear your old tennis shoes," she said, "For that's too far to walk barefooted."

"Even for you," Martha teased.

"Yes, even for me."

By the time we reached my uncle's house about three quarters of a mile from ours, they were all ready and seemingly waiting on us. I wondered why they hadn't driven down to get us to save us that extra walking, but I said nothing. Uncle Albert and Henry were on horseback and Roxanne was in the car. She was just Elizabeth's age, but was already driving. She told us to get in with her to ride to the pasture and we did. I liked her better than I did Henry, but I always felt it was unfair that they had so much and we had so little. At least, that's what Elizabeth was always saying.

At the pasture, they opened a big gate and drove the herd of cattle out onto the road. Bowzer, their black dog, was helping by snapping at their heels. These were beef cattle that would be sold later so they wanted them to eat a lot of grass this summer to fatten them up. There were probably thirty to fifty of them. They kept moving about so much I couldn't count them exactly.

We got out of the car, even Roxanne did, to help get them started down the road. Then Uncle Albert gave Martha and me each a big stick and told us to walk one on either side of the road to keep them from straying into the fields. He and Henry came behind us on horseback and Roxanne followed driving slowly in the car.

At first, it was fun and seemed like an adventure, but soon I felt hot and tired, and my feet hurt, and it wasn't fun at all. Most of the cows followed one another without too much trouble, but a few were stubborn like our Susie, and tried to take off on their own. These were the ones we had to chase. I was glad when Roxanne suggested that I ride with her in the car for awhile.

When we came to a creek, most of the cows went down into the water for a cool drink, but a few wandered off even then and we had to go bring them back. I was thirsty myself and was glad when Roxanne got a big jug of water out of the car and gave us all drinks. I wanted to throw myself down on the soft grass and rest awhile, but Uncle Albert said that we couldn't let the cattle linger too long, or they would get restless.

The sun got hotter, the cattle more stubborn, and my feet more tired. It felt like a blister was coming on my heel. Martha rode for awhile a couple of times, and I felt like a real martyr as I struggled along alone forgetting that I had ridden in the car much more than she had. The only thing that kept me going was the thought of getting paid for all this, and by that time I had it up to five dollars for each of us.

Finally, when we reached a vacant field with plenty of shade trees, we stopped to let the cattle rest and we sat under the trees and ate our lunches. As usual, I thought that theirs looked better than ours, but since I was hungry, gratefully ate what Mom had fixed. When I had finished,

I stretched out and closed my eyes. But when Henry, who had been riding a horse all morning, said scornfully, "Too young and tender for a cattle drive, eh?" I immediately sat up.

"No, I'm fine," I answered while my dislike for him grew more. And for the rest of the drive I bravely tried to walk as far as I could before riding in the car.

At the highway, we had real trouble, and even Roxanne had to get out of the car and help as some of the cows got spooked and took off in the wrong direction. It could have been a real catastrophe if the cars hadn't completely stopped and waited until we rounded up the strays and got them all safely across. All of us were hot and tired and cross by the time this was accomplished.

But fortunately we were soon at their other pasture and our mission was over. I breathed a sigh of relief as the last cow straggled through the gate and plunged down the creek for a drink. Uncle Albert fastened up the gate and turned to Roxanne.

"You ride Rowdy back and I'll take the girls home."

"Ok," she agreed quickly. Then she added, "Dad, Let Bowzer ride in the car please for he's awful tired."

I was glad that she said this for the dog did look tired as he stood with his pink tongue hanging out of his mouth while he panted incessantly.

"Sure," he agreed. "Looks like he needs a drink too." He took the water jug and poured some water in the lid to let the thirsty animal lap it up. Then he ordered him into the front seat of the car while Martha and I crawled wearily into the back. All the way home, I thought about the money we were going to receive and planned ways I would spend it.

When we got back to his house, he said, "I have a special treat for you boys for being such good helpers," and I thought maybe he was going to give us ten dollars each. But then he added, "Come on out to the barn and we'll get it."

Martha and I looked at each other in surprise and wonder, but we followed him silently to the barn where he opened a stable door and we saw a little white goat. "Isn't this a fine goat? I've decided to give it to you for being such good helpers. What do you think of that?"

Speechless we stared at the goat wondering all the while what Mom and Daddy were going to say about that. But Uncle Albert just tied a rope around its neck and led it over to his old pickup that stood in the barn lot. He lifted it up into the back of the truck and motioned us to follow. "You better ride up here with it so it doesn't fall out," he said, and we did what he said. All the way home, we just looked at each other and didn't know what to say. I kept thinking about the money I had so counted on, and remembering that Grandma was always saying, "Don't count your chickens until they hatch." But I did think it might be exciting to have a goat.

Mom seemed as surprised as we were when he unloaded us and the goat. But she seemed as cowered of Uncle Albert as we were and she said nothing. And she was very fond of most animals and the goat was so cute.

He was getting back in the truck when as an afterthought, he reached in his pocket and pulled out some money. He handed it to Martha saying, "Share it with your sister, but you should have more for you walked the most," and without a word of thanks for all our hard labor, he was gone.

Martha opened her hand and we all stared at the money. There was a dollar bill and three quarters which meant only a dollar seventy-five for the both of us. Seeing the disappointment in Martha's eyes, I insisted that she keep the dollar and I take the seventy-five cents for I knew that she had walked more and worked harder, and I would probably enjoy the goat more than she would. Walking over to the little white animal, I got down on my knees and put my arms around its neck hiding my disappointment for all the money I had planned to get. A goat and seventy-five cents for a cattle drive! Would that even atone for my blisters?

Chapter 9

Christmas Program

The goat was a cute little thing and we all fell in love with her except Mom who thought she was a nuisance from the very beginning. But she didn't say much for when they talked about the patience of Job in Sunday School, I always thought they were talking about my mother. We called the goat Nanny and enjoyed playing with her, but Mom insisted that she be kept in the pigpen with the pigs, and no sooner would we put her in there then she would jump out.

Soon school started and this year I was in fifth grade, but still by myself. Everyone seemed happy because Mr. Birkey was back. He had taught in our school for five years before I started, and Naomi, Joey, and Martha liked him while Elizabeth, who thought school was wonderful, claimed that he was the best teacher ever. I liked school too and looked forward to a good year. This would be the year that I would put my dream into words, and this would be the year that the most terrible war that could be dreamed of would begin.

Naomi had gotten married this past summer to a young fellow in the army named Larry, and they were living in Kentucky. I missed her very much and felt jealous of her love for her new husband. But she sent me special cards and I knew that she still loved me.

I soon found that Mr. Birkey, though very strict who put up with nonsense from no one, was a good teacher, and I loved school more than ever. Ellen and Martha were in eighth grade so it made me sad that they would be gone to high school next year. The other Ginny was in sixth grade and we were still special friends.

Fall went by as usual with our softball games with other schools, the annual box supper and wiener roast, and before we knew it, it was December again. It was time to make plans for Christmas. We always had a program and a big Christmas tree, but Elizabeth, who was now a senior in high school at Carmen, had told me that Mr. Birkey would see that we had a bigger taller tree, a bigger better program, and the most delicious treats that I could imagine. So, you can imagine my excitement when we turned the calendar on the kitchen wall at home to December.

And sure enough the very next day Mr. Birkey stood up before the school after lunch and said, "This afternoon I am going to take the bigger boys out to the woods to find us a Christmas tree. Any of the rest of you that want to come along can, but if some of you little ones want to stay here, I've asked Martha and Ellen to stay with you and play games." Teachers could do those things in those days too.

I didn't consider myself little, but I certainly wanted to go, and it turned out that all the little ones were eager to be a part of the fun, even fussy little Milly Jean so we all donned our wraps and took off for the woods with Mr. Birkey leading the way carrying his big axe.

We yelled and shouted as we tramped through the woods looking for the biggest, most perfect cedar tree in the world to take back to our classroom. Everyone was in a good mood except Milly Jean who complained all the way that she was tired, or cold, or something. No one paid much attention to her despite the fact that her father was one of the three school directors in the days before school boards, and the teachers usually catered to her every wish.

Suddenly, I saw it towering over the other bushes and small trees over to the right—a tall cedar that seemed to touch the sky. "There it is!" I shouted. "There's the perfect one." And everyone, even the teacher, stopped and came back to look.

But Martha, who was always afraid that I would embarrass her, was already calling, "It's probably too big, Mr. Birkey. Ginny does get so carried away."

"It's way too big," said Jack Andrews, one of the eighth grade boys, and my heart sank.

But Mr. Birkey, who was a big man himself, tall and also quite stout as it wasn't nice to call someone fat, stopped and looked at the tree, walking around it to look carefully at every side, then squinted his eyes for the afternoon sun was peeping through just there, and finally, to my delight, said, "It has a beautiful shape and if it's too tall, we can cut more off the bottom. Ginny, I think you have found our perfect tree."

I couldn't help smiling smugly at Martha and Jack Andrews as the teacher and older boys took turns chopping at the trunk of the tree, my beautiful, beautiful tree. We always had little ones at home and we had never had one this big at school.

That night I shared my excitement and delight with Elizabeth while she was doing her English assignment at the kitchen table. She stopped working and put her arm around me to give me a hug. "Ginny, that's wonderful," she said. "You know, I think you share my romantic nature."

"What does that mean?" I asked for I was always trying to figure out the big words that she liked to use.

"It means that we have a vivid imagination, we get excited about things, and we're fond of making up fanciful stories."

"Is that good?" I asked.

"Of course," she answered. "Why, maybe someday you'll be a great story writer and poet like me." Then she turned back to her work, lifting her eyes one last time to me. "Now, scoot. I've an important story to write."

Then as I backed out of the kitchen, she called after me, "Wait til you see those sacks of treats he'll bring on

program night. You've never seen anything like it." And then I was so excited that I thought I'd never go to sleep.
Next day Mr. Birkey brought a big wooden stand that he had made for the tree, then he cut off enough of the trunk that when they stood it at the front of the room, the top almost touched the ceiling. We made paper chains out of red and green paper, strung popcorn and red haws from the hawthorn tree to hang around the tree, and we made ornaments out of red and gold liners from coffee bags that Chester Aston's mother had saved for us. But when all of these were hung in place then the greatest surprise came. Mr. Birkey brought out strings of real lights, glass ornaments, and store bought icicles to put on the tree. When he turned off the lights, and plugged in the tree lights, I thought it was the most beautiful thing I had ever seen in my life.

Before Thanksgiving we had been assigned our parts for the program so we would have a long time to learn them. All the little kids had pieces to recite, even some of the older ones did too including me. I loved to do that type of thing and had a real long one that I already knew. The little kids as a group would sing "Up on the Housetop" and "Jolly Old St. Nicholas" while the whole school would close the program with "Silent Night" as we could sing religious songs at school programs back then.

Besides all of that and Santa coming at the end of the program to pass out the presents and treats, we always did some plays, usually two or three short ones that we school kids performed, and one big long one that some of the high school kids were in and sometimes even some of the adults in the community like Ellen's uncle who often played an old man. I had desperately wanted to be in one of the long plays and I felt that surely that I was old enough and that this would be my year.

So, on that Monday night before Thanksgiving when Elizabeth and Martha got ready to go to the schoolhouse for the tryouts, I begged to go too.

"You don't need to go, Ginny," said Martha scornfully. "This play is for the older kids and those in the community that want to be in it. You know that Mr. Birkey told the little kids not to come."

"But I'm not a little kid," I retorted.

And Martha who was usually so kind, snapped back, "Well, you're not a big kid either."

"No, I'm just halfway so why can't I be included with the big kids?"

"Because you're—"

But Elizabeth who was pulling on a clean sweater over her blonde head said, "Oh, Martha, let her come. It can't do any harm."

I flashed her a warm smile and ran to ask Mom if I could go. She too seemed to have doubts. "I think it's just for the older kids, honey," she said while she dumped the skillet full of popped corn into a big dishpan on the back of the stove. "Why don't you just stay here with us and enjoy this good popcorn?"

"No, Mom, I want to go," I insisted. "Elizabeth said that I could even though Martha is being stubborn. Please let me go."

GINNY'S DREAM

"Why, Ginny?" she asked.

"Because I want to be in the big play this year," I answered.

"You want to be in the big play?" She seemed greatly surprised. I watched as she put a big spoonful of lard in the hot skillet and as soon as it melted, she poured in some more freshly shelled popcorn that Daddy had shelled into a bowl while he sat in his favorite rocker behind the heating stove. She flopped on the lid and shook the skillet by the long handle a few times then she turned her attention back to me. "But, Ginny, you know that the big play is mostly for high school kids and other people in the community with only a few parts going to the older kids in school. You're only in fifth grade."

"I know, Mom, but there is a part that I know I can do. Please let me go."

"Well, all right if Elizabeth doesn't mind, but do behave and don't embarrass Martha. And put on your warm wraps for that wind sounds cold." She turned back to the popcorn and I ran for the bedroom.

Soon tightly bundled up, we hurried down the road. Ellen and her Uncle Willie, who was trying out for a part again this year, were waiting for us by the mailbox. We exchanged greetings and went on up the west road bracing ourselves against the strong wind. The schoolhouse looked warm and bright with the electric lights shining out in the darkness. We hung up our wraps in the cloakroom and went on into the classroom. Several people were already there, and others came as we did so within five minutes, Mr. Birkey had called everyone to attention, and the tryouts began.

I sat down to watch and crossed my fingers for luck. How I wanted to be in that play! In third grade, Rex Harper and I had been twins in a little play and we had to wear our pajamas as we were waiting up for Santa Claus. I didn't have any pajamas as I always slept in a gown, but Vivian agreed to make me some when Mom explained our problem to her. Last year we did a religious play because Mr. Gordon's father was a preacher and his mother wrote the play, and I had got to be part of the group at the inn where there was no room for Jesus. But never had I even been considered for the big play and I wanted to be in it so badly.

Martha and Elizabeth both tried out for parts and so did Ellen though I knew that she really didn't want to be in it. Some of the other high school girls also tried out and then Milly Jean Aston's mother came dragging that little snotty- nosed kid with her. The girls all looked at each other in disappointment for they knew she'd get the part because her husband was one of the directors who hired and fired the teachers. But Mr. Birkey never seemed to be buffaloed by them, and lo and behold, he gave that part to Elizabeth.

Then suddenly the teacher looked at me still sitting there in the front desk with my fingers still tightly crossed. "Ginny," he said, and when I lifted my head to him, he asked, "Are you just here to watch, or did you want to try out for a part?"

I tried to answer, but couldn't get the words to come out so I cleared my throat and could finally speak. "I want to try out, Mr. Birkey. I know that I can do it."

"And what part did you want to try out for?" he asked kindly.

"The poor lady who has no food or presents for her children," I answered, and Martha glared at me for that was the part that she had tried out for earlier.

Then to my great surprise, he held a copy of the play out to me and said, "Go ahead. Elizabeth, you read your part with her."

With my heart thudding and my hands damp, I took the coveted papers and stepped up on the platform and read the part in a loud confident voice. I think even Martha was amazed, Elizabeth, who was playing the rich lady that came on Christmas Eve to bring me the needed food and presents, gave me a quick hug, and Uncle Willie, who was always one of my favorite people, flashed me a smile from across the room. He had already gotten the part of the old grandfather who the poor lady also had to take care of.

But Mr. Birkey just took the play back, and then had Martha and one of the high school girls try it again. Knowing I had done a good job, I went back to my seat so confident that I didn't even cross my fingers this time, or even say a quick prayer as I was so prone to do. Therefore, it was with great surprise that I heard the teacher say, "I think Martha does the best job so she gets the part. We'll try out the other boy parts now so you girls can leave if you want to."

GINNY'S DREAM

Somehow, I got to my feet and stumbled after the others out to the cloakroom where we put on our wraps. Then when Uncle Willie opened the outside door, we went out into the night which as Mom had predicted was suddenly much colder. Elizabeth and Martha were both delighted that they had gotten the parts, and kept saying over and over, "I got it. I really did." I felt very angry and sad, but I didn't say anything, and I don't think they really understood how disappointed I was. But after we parted from Ellen and her uncle at the mailbox, I suddenly began to cry and then they knew. Elizabeth stopped and knelt on the cold ground to put her arms around me.

"Oh, Ginny, you really wanted that part, didn't you?" And at my muffled sob of agreement, she went on, "I'm sorry, Punkin," using Daddy's nickname for me, "But you'll get another chance when you're older."

I realized then that Martha was sorry too for her hands were patting my back and she was saying, "You did do a good job, Ginny. Please don't cry so." And I did stop crying before we reached the house, but the hurt stayed. Maybe that was one reason that I was so thrilled when Mr. Birkey chose the Christmas tree that I had found, and I claimed it as my very own while I stared at its beauty.

Then on Sunday night, which was December 7, 1941, as we listened to the news on our new battery radio, we heard the terrible announcement that the Japanese had bombed Pearl Harbor, and that our country was at war. We sat in a stunned group around the radio while fear gripped our hearts. I was afraid that they would come and bomb us, but my mother's fear was that Joey would have to go fight, and I think we all realized that Naomi's new husband was already in the army and would be sure to go. Somehow, the radio didn't seem so wonderful after all for if we hadn't had it, we wouldn't have known that awful news. At least, not that night. But since it was there, we stayed glued to it until bedtime. As I said my prayers, the thought came to me that maybe Mr. Birkey would cancel the whole program, the treats and everything, and that seemed more than I could bear. So, I threw in a special plea for that not to be.

I thought my prayers did some good for next morning, Mr. Birkey announced that we would go on with the program as planned for he felt that everyone would need some cheering up. The next step was to build a big stage. One of the fathers came to school that week with a lot of long boards in his pickup truck and with Mr. Birkey and the bigger boys' help, he built a huge stage that covered the small platform where the teacher's desk usually set and stretched from one side of the room to the other. There was hammering for several days, before and after school, and sometimes even while we worked on our assignments.

Martha and Ellen would often take the little kids to the back of the room to help them with their numbers, or listen to them read. I longed to do that, and I think it was during that time and later when we practiced for the program and they did the same thing that my dream became a reality. I suddenly knew that I wanted to be a teacher when I grew up. I thought it would be great to help boys and girls to learn, and I could put on the most wonderful Christmas program in the world. I still wanted to be a writer, but I figured that if I were a teacher that I could write too. Why, I could even write the plays for the program.

When the stage was built, some mothers came to measure, and then they sewed together white sheets which they strung up on the wires that Mr. Birkey had hung all across the front and sides of the stage. Now, we had curtains just like professionals. Oh, how I wished I could have been the poor lady in the big play!

Now, that all of this was done we began to practice for our program every day. We rushed through our lessons in the mornings, and worked on our assignments in the afternoons, or we were supposed to, while the others practiced. They practiced the big play at night so I didn't have to watch that. But I listened when Martha and Elizabeth practiced at home and I soon knew both of their parts. And sometimes I begged to go along and just watch, and I learned all of the actions as well. It turned out that it was a good thing that I did.

The program was scheduled for the 23rd on Tuesday night before Christmas. Then we would be on vacation until after New Year's Day. Martha, who was always getting sore throats, felt like she was coming down with a cold on Friday the 19th, but she went on to school anyway for she was a good student and never liked to miss. And besides, they were having their last practice that night for the big play, "Christmas Gifts," and she couldn't miss that. So, she didn't tell Mom how badly she felt that night, or she would never have let her go out in the cold. By the time, she and Elizabeth got back from practice, she was really sick. Her face was flushed and she could hardly talk.

Daddy and the little girls were already asleep, but Mom and I were sitting close to the heating stove with the light from the kerosene lamp on the library table casting a rosy glow on our books. It was a new lamp that Naomi had brought when she came home to visit this past fall. It was called an Aladdin lamp and had a tall chimney and a mantle that glowed from the heat and gave a much better light than the old kerosene lamps. It was almost as good as having electricity. We were both reading library books that I had brought home from school for she loved to read as much as I did. I was reading Island of the Red God, and she was reading Dickeon Among the Indians.

We both looked up when the door opened, and when Mom saw Martha's flushed face, she got up quickly and went over to her. "What's the matter, Martha? You look like you are sick."

Martha just nodded her head and began taking off her wraps, but Elizabeth said, "She is. I think she has a fever and she can hardly talk."

Mom's hand went to Martha's forehead, as always her test for fever, and drew back quickly while she exclaimed, "You're burning up." Then in reproach, "You shouldn't have gone out tonight."

"But I had to go to the practice," Martha responded in a barely audible voice as she sank down in Mom's rocker, and put her head in her hands.

Elizabeth and I helped her get undressed and into bed while Mom got a washpan of cold water and a washcloth to bathe her flushed face and some aspirin to bring down the fever. In the morning she was no better.

She was still sick on Monday so despite her protests, Mom kept her home from school. When Mr. Birkey checked the attendance, he spoke to me sharply, "Ginny, where is Martha?"

"She's sick."

"Sick? How sick?"

"Very sick. She has a fever and she cannot talk."

"CANNOT TALK?" the teacher shouted, and everyone in the room looked up. "But what are we going to do about her part in the play tomorrow night?"

"I guess someone else will have to do it," I answered.

"And who might that someone be at this late date?" and I noticed that Ellen was already shaking her head, and so was the other Ginny.

"Me," I said in a small voice hardly daring to lift my head.

"But you can't learn the part in that short of time," he argued.

"I already know it."

"You do?"

"Yes."

"All of it?"

Now, I lifted my head and spoke bravely, "Yes, all of it, and also all of the things that she is supposed to do. Please let me do it, Mr. Birkey."

GINNY'S DREAM

So, after having Ellen read through the parts with me to show him that I did indeed know it, the coveted part was actually mine. But somehow it turned out to be a bittersweet victory for I knew that Martha would be terribly disappointed. But she was back to her usual sweet self and when I told her she just hugged me and said in a whisper, "I'm glad you got it, Ginny. Do a good job."

I was so excited when the next night came that I could hardly breathe. Martha was better, even though she still couldn't talk, and Mom gave in to her pleading to go to the program. We all bundled up in our wraps, and Daddy took us in the wagon. When we got there, the schoolhouse was all lit up and it seemed that everyone in the community had come. Suddenly, I felt very scared, and just knew I couldn't do it, but Elizabeth put her hand on my shoulder and said with a big smile, "You'll do fine, Ginny. I just know you will."

But it seemed such a long time to get to the big play. I made it through my long piece, and my short part in one of the little plays. Then we were behind the curtains pulling on our costumes, and I heard the teacher announcing the big play. Elizabeth gave me a gentle push and I found myself on stage. At first, I was terribly scared, but then I thought to myself, "You wanted this and now you've got it. This is your big chance to show what you can do." And I did. I knew that I did a good job though few people then would tell you so, but I felt real satisfaction at a job well done, and the audience gave us lots of applause. I decided then that maybe I'd be an actress instead of a teacher.

GINNY'S DREAM

The whole program had gone well, even the singing. We sang besides the Christmas songs "My Country Tis of Thee," and "God Bless America," because of the war, but even Mr. Birkey knew better than to have us try "The Star Spangled Banner." Our voices were just not that good.

It was fun and excitement when Santa came rushing in with his pack on his bag, even though we knew it was Randall Spencer, except for the little kids, of course, who really thought it was Santa. He gave out our gifts from our having drawn names a couple of weeks ago. Chester Aston had my name, and his mother had bought me the book Black Beauty, and nothing could have made me happier.

Then the teacher had Santa pass out our treats, a small paper sack for each of us, and when I looked in mine, I knew that Elizabeth had been right about Mr. Birkey for there inside the sack was an orange, a big red apple, some hard Christmas candy and some chocolate drops, and, in my mind, the best candy in the world—chocolate covered peanut clusters. I thought that Mr. Birkey must be rich, or maybe Santa had actually brought the treats for how could he manage all of this for everyone on just seventy-five dollars a month?

Then two days later on Christmas morning, I had two more surprises. Naomi had sent me a very special gift. It was a little merry-go-round with a top and horses and everything, and when you wound it up, it went round and round. I was so happy that I almost cried. Then when I opened my next gift, I did cry just a little bit. It was a china peacock with a long tail, and it was just from Daddy alone. He had never given me a gift before and even at ten years old I was touched. He had worked for a neighbor shucking corn, and he had saved some of the money to buy each of us a little gift. It had indeed been a wonderful Christmas time.

Chapter 10

Babies

I was almost eleven years old when I first learned about babies. I don't mean how they are made, or even how they are born, but just that someone was going to have a baby. No one said the word "pregnant" in those early days of the forties. They sometimes said that someone was expecting, or that they were going to have a baby. Well, this someone was someone pretty special, and not just anyone. It was my own mom, who I thought was way too old to have babies. Why, she was almost forty years old!

It was a warm afternoon in early spring, and my older sister and I were sitting on top of the wooden gate that separated the potato patch from the barn lot. She had said that she wanted to tell me something important so we had gone as far from the house as possible. Her news had nearly knocked me off the fence. I stared at her in disbelief.

"Are you sure?" I just couldn't believe that my mother was going to have another baby. There were seven of us already, not counting the little brother who had died when he was only a few weeks old. Surely, that was enough for any family. At least, I knew it was for ours. "Are you sure?" I asked again.

Martha was three years older than me, and she looked at me now with all the superiority of her thirteen years. "Yes, I am sure, Ginny. I am very sure."

"But who told you?" I asked still unable to believe. "Who told you that Mom was going to have a baby?"

"She did herself," Martha replied with a smugness that I hated. "She told me and asked me to tell you so you wouldn't be asking questions."

"What kind of questions? Why would I ask questions? I don't even know any questions to ask."

"Haven't you noticed that Mom is getting real big in her stomach? Surely, you have noticed that."

I bent my dark head for a moment in thought. Then I lifted my head and looked up at my sister. "Yes, I had noticed that, but I thought she was just getting fat. What does that have to do with having a baby?"

"That's where she carries the baby, silly."

"Really? How does it get there?" This was getting harder to believe all the time.

Martha stared at me for a long time. I thought that I caught a glimpse of a smile in her green eyes which were the same shade as mine. Then she said as she placed a hand on my shoulder. "You're too young to know that now. I'll tell you when you are older. Now, don't tell anyone about the baby and don't ask a lot of stupid questions." She slid off the gate and started for the house.

I jumped down and ran after her. "When will the baby be born? Do you know that?"

"Of course," she answered scornfully as though everyone knew. "About the middle of June." Then she went on toward the house.

I walked slowly back to the gate and climbed up on top of it where I sat lost in thought. I could barely remember when Janice was born when I was four years old. That was when Daddy was so sick in the hospital and Mom was so sad and we all had to work so hard to have enough to eat. Then I really remembered three years ago when another little sister had been born—the one who had gone without a name for nearly a week until finally Daddy had held her up in his arms and suggested that we call her Alice after his daughter by another wife who had died just before I was born. Both times we had been awakened in the middle of the night and taken down to our cousin Vivian's to stay the rest of the night. I wondered if this would happen again when this new baby came.

Slowly, I climbed down from the gate and began to walk toward the house turning this new information over and over in my mind. So, doctors didn't bring babies in their big black bags like some of the kids at school said after all. They were inside their mother's stomachs. But how did they get there and how did they get out of there? Those were questions that my small mind could not grasp and understand.

When I entered the kitchen, Mom was already fixing supper. She smiled at me, but said nothing. Martha had begun my sex education and she would be the one though the years that would finish it. I often wondered if there had been no Martha if Mom would have told me herself.

I couldn't help stealing glances at her stomach. She wore an apron as usual, but I couldn't help noticing that it was much bigger than usual. It was still hard for me to imagine that there was a baby inside. It just seemed impossible. I knew that I was staring, but couldn't help it.

"Ginny, it's time to do your chores." My mother's voice interrupted my thoughts, and I didn't know how many times she had called to me. But she only smiled as I looked up at her and nodded my head in reply.

From as far back as I could remember, I had followed at my father's heels, or ridden on his lap while he disked, or plowed the fields, gone with him in the wagon to cut or gather firewood, and helped him with the chores in the barn. So, it was to the big barn that I now ran, ready to help him as usual. He was already up in the hayloft throwing down hay in the mangers for the cows and horses who were in their stalls waiting to be fed.

"About time," he said as my head appeared at the top of the ladder. But he smiled, and I knew that he was not angry. My father was usually a quiet gentle man, and since his illness had retired more and more into himself, letting my mother and older brother take control. But sometimes, he got really upset so I always tried to keep him in a good mood.

As I helped him throw down the hay, and then walk through the mangers giving each of the animals two or three ears of dried corn, I wondered if he knew about the new baby. But times were still hard and sometimes there was not enough money for the things we needed, so I decided not to be the one to break the news to him about another mouth to feed.

"I think it's about warm enough to disk up the potato patch," he said, and I nodded in reply, but the words potato patch reminded me of the astounding news I had heard there this afternoon. Again, I wondered about telling him, and again I decided not to.

He let me carry the corn out to the pigpen where I threw it out to the big sows who came running with their funny little pigs following close behind. By the time I got back to the barn, he had begun the milking. He had started on Susie, the big reddish cow, who was always so stubborn about driving in from the pasture, because he knew that I liked to milk Old Jersey who was always gentle and quiet and could be milked from either side.

"Be sure you get every drop," he reminded me as I sat down on a stool and put the bucket under Old Jersey's udders. "You know how your mom gets her redheaded dander up if we don't strip the cows right."

"Okay, Daddy, I'll be real careful." I smiled to myself as I watched the spurts of milk gush into the bucket. He liked to tease Mom, and sometimes she did fuss about getting every last drop of milk for it was not good for the cows to not get it all, but we all knew that they loved each other and they didn't fuss and fight.

Then I heard him chuckle and I raised my head. "Ready for your supper, are you?" he called to the cats who lived in the barn and came down at milking time for a taste of the warm fresh milk. Though he always poured some in a big pan that set in the entry way, he liked to give them a treat beforehand. I watched with pleasure as he raised the cow's teat and sprayed some milk toward their waiting open mouths. After each had had a taste, he went back to filling the bucket. Humming to himself, he quickly finished and stripped the cow until not even a trickle of milk came out. Then he stood and came over to me.

"Let me finish Jersey and you go fill the wood box. It'll soon be time for supper." As I stood up and started for the house, he called after me, "Don't forget the kindling. It's too warm to keep the fires going all night."

And I didn't say a word about the baby, I thought to myself. I wonder if he knows.

I wondered the same thing next day at school. I wondered if my best friend, whose name was also Ginny and who was a year older than me, knew about babies, and especially if she knew about my mom. But I didn't dare say anything for fear she didn't know. It was like telling someone about Santa Claus, or the Easter Bunny, and maybe they didn't know.

My next best friend, who was sometimes my best considering the moods we were in, was Ellen. I figured that she probably knew for she was the same age as Martha, even a month older, but still I was afraid to ask. And besides, I couldn't get a moment with her when Martha wasn't around, and I had in a way promised Martha that I wouldn't say anything, or ask any questions. So, I just wondered and wondered, and said nothing to anyone.

I got to run in the track meet again, and this time I won a blue ribbon. I ran all the way home so filled with excitement that I could hardly wait to show Mom. As usual, she was happy and excited for me too. I thought that she looked tired, and she probably was, and I began to worry that she would die when the baby was born. I wondered how we could ever manage without her, and felt very sad. In all this time, it never occurred to me that she'd already had eight children and had lived through the birth of all of them. I was so afraid that she would die. I tried to pray about it, but it seemed that the words just wouldn't come.

Soon school was out for another summer vacation, and I tried to help Mom more than I usually did. Our Nanny goat had become a real problem, and none of us seemed to know what to do. In the wintertime, we had kept her in the barn at night so she'd be warm, and put her out in the pasture with the cows in the daytime. If she jumped the fence, and ran about over the farm, it was no big deal. But now that the pigs had been moved back out to their pen, and Nanny wouldn't stay either in the pigpen, or the pasture, she became a real nuisance.

My five year old sister Janice added to the problem for she was always afraid that the goat was going to get hurt, and spent much of her time weeping and wailing. One warm May morning she came dashing in the kitchen where Mom was cooking navy beans in one big pot on the kitchen range and wild greens that she had gathered by the roadside in another one while she stirred up a big bowl of cornbread. Martha was setting the table and I was sweeping the old faded linoleum. In my dreams, I was always going to buy Mom nice and pretty things when I got rich, and one of these would be a new linoleum I had already decided. Now, Janice brought us all up short by her screaming.

"Mom, come quick," she was yelling though we could barely make out what she was saying for she was crying so hard.

All of us dropped what we were doing and ran outside, expecting the worse—the house on fire, or little Alice being attacked by a mad dog—only to find it was Nanny causing the concern. The white goat stood perched on the half open cover of the cistern where water was stored for our use. It was a precarious position indeed and we all felt concern, but it was soon apparent to us that while Janice was just afraid that the goat would fall off and be hurt, Mom was more concerned that it might fall in the cistern and ruin our water. Very carefully Martha and I pushed our pet off the cover so she landed in the yard. Then we pushed the top over enough to cover the cistern, and tried to calm Janice. We all tried to be extra careful about keeping it covered, but Nanny found this a favorite perch, and Janice spent many hours screaming that Nanny was going to fall and get hurt.

That she had another favorite perch and one that also brought screams of fright from Janice was made known to us the very next week. Aunt Marie had come to visit and we were gathered in the living room talking when we heard Janice yelling.

Mom turned to me and said, "Ginny, go get Nanny off the cistern so she will stop that noise."

"Janice is so silly," I said to myself as I went through to the kitchen and out the back door. But there was no goat on the cistern cover and Janice was nowhere in sight. But I could still hear her so I went around the house, and there in the side yard was Aunt Marie's car and on top of the car stood Nanny as proudly as though she were a king. Janice was running around and around the car with Alice trailing her screaming at the top of her lungs.

When she saw me, Janice stopped crying long enough to say, "Make her get down, Ginny 'fore she falls and gets killed."

"She won't get killed, Janice, so do be quiet." I was much more concerned, as Mom would be later when she found out the trouble, that the goat would harm the car. But I climbed up on the running board, stretched up to reach the goat's legs and pushed. She leaped nimbly down onto the hood and then to the ground. I grabbed her by the scuff of the neck and dragged her to the pigpen. Fortunately, she stayed there until after Aunt Marie left.

After this happened two or three times, and the last time to a neighbor who wasn't very nice about it, not that we could blame him, Mom warned us that it had better not happen again, or the goat would go back to Uncle Albert. I didn't want to worry her for I was still very much afraid that she might die when the baby came, and I didn't want to give up the goat so whenever anyone came, I took Nanny to the barn and locked her in a stall until they left.

Last summer I had joined the 4-H club which was led by one of our neighbors and good friends, Hattie Austin, who lived across the creek and up the north road. There were only girls in ours and it was a cooking club. This summer since we were in war, our project was to have a Victory Garden where we would raise food, harvest and can it ourselves as extra food for next winter. It was no big deal for Martha and me for we had always had to help in Mom's garden, but those little plots of garden that were just ours did become kind of special. And we did have fun in the club. Betsy and Ginny stopped by to pick up Ellen then came by our house and we all went to Hattie's together where her two cousins from a nearby school and church community joined us.

Our meetings were on Wednesday afternoons so on that hot June day, Martha and I had just gotten ready when the other girls arrived. I had noticed that Mom had continued to get bigger and bigger since Martha had told me that she was going to have a baby. And sometimes she lay down in the afternoon to rest, or said that she had a headache. I kissed her good-by that afternoon when we left and told her that I loved her.

When we got home, Mom was lying down on her bed, and she asked us to finish supper.

"What's wrong with her?" I asked my sister when we got to the kitchen.

"It's time for the baby to be born," Martha answered matter-of-factly.

"How do you know that?"

"Because she told me, and besides you have a baby after nine months, and it's been nine months."

"Martha, does Daddy know that she's going to have a baby?" I had to know the answer to that question.

Martha stared at me for a few moments then she laughed. "Yes, Ginny, he knows. Just trust me."

She went on slicing potatoes to fry while I cleaned the leaf lettuce and radishes. Then I asked the question that had been uppermost in my mind for these many weeks. "Martha, is she going to die? Is Mom going to die?"

My sister laid down her knife and came to put her arms around me. "No, Ginny, she is not going to die. She will be in a lot of pain and she may cry out, but she won't die."

Mom came to the table for some supper then she laid back down. But by the time we were through with the dishes, she was walking from room to room her face grimaced in pain. I ran to her and threw my arms around her thick middle.

"Mom, what's wrong?" I asked in alarm.

"It's just the baby, Ginny. It's ready to be born, and the pains can be pretty bad for awhile." Then she turned to my father who was sitting in the living room listening to the radio. "Joe, it's time."

"Time for what?"

"Time to call the doctor. And Ginny, it's time for you to take Janice and Alice down to Milly's. You're going to spend the night with Ellen, and Milly is going to come help the doctor. Would you go now before it gets too dark?" Then as though she read the fear in my eyes, she added, "Don't worry, Ginny, I'll be all right."

"Are you coming with us, Martha?" I asked as I turned to go get my little sisters.

"No, I'm staying here to help. You're helping too, Ginny, by taking the little ones. So, just go and don't fuss."

I wanted to stay too and didn't want to leave, but neither did I want to worry Mom so I gathered up our nightgowns and toothbrushes, and took my little sisters down to Milly's.

I kept worrying about Mom and praying that she wouldn't die so I didn't enjoy the games that we played, or the radio programs we listened to. I didn't even enjoy the candy that Uncle Willie brought back to us when he came home from town. Finally, it was time to go to bed. I helped Ellen fix pallets for Janice and Alice on the floor then I crawled into bed beside her, but I couldn't go to sleep.

It was almost morning when I heard Milly close the front door and come into the house. She came to our bedroom door and I sat up in bed instantly.

"How's my mom?" I asked in a scared voice.

"Oh, she's fine, Ginny," Milly answered in her cheerful way. "And guess what? You have a new baby brother. Isn't that nice?"

"Yes, that's really nice," I answered, but the old fear and doubt was still there. "Are you sure my mom is all right?"

"Yes, very sure."

I crawled out of bed and put my arms around Milly's waist. "Could I go home, Milly? I really want to see for myself."

"Can't you wait until morning, Ginny? I'm really very tired, and your mother is probably asleep."

"No, I need to go now. I'll go by myself. I'm not afraid."

"Get dressed and I'll take you," she said and suddenly her voice was not so tired. "But leave the little ones here."

So, I dressed quickly and Ellen didn't even wake up. Soon, hand in hand, we hurried up the road, and when Martha answered the door, Milly said, "Ginny couldn't wait until morning to see her new brother so here she is."

Martha took me into the bedroom where I went to Mom's bed and put my arms around her to make sure that she was all right. She sleepily gave me a quick hug, and then Martha was holding out to me the baby wrapped in a blanket. His face was red and wrinkled, and his eyes were crinkled up as he cried, but I thought he was beautiful and I loved him. Maybe having a baby wasn't so bad after all.

Chapter 11

Dollar A Day

It was fun taking care of the baby for a few days, but that wore off pretty fast. Martha, who was only thirteen years old, had taken over the running of the house, doing the cooking, cleaning, laundry—which meant scrubbing clothes on the board, and caring for Mom who had to stay in bed for ten days, so I had to help. But I didn't really enjoy doing all that work and I was glad when Mom was up and about, and I wasn't needed all that much. I liked to rock the baby, who we had named Ross, when I wanted to, and not when I had to.

Mom had been up for a few days and was nursing the baby in the living room one afternoon while I finished washing the dinner dishes. Martha was scrubbing clothes, standing on the ground with the washtub on the back porch, when a car pulled up beside the house. I quickly dried my hands and ran out the back door to go take Nanny to lock her in the barn.

When I came back to the house and went into the living room, I saw that our visitors were the Lawrence "girls" as everyone called them even though they were older than my mom. We also called them old maids as they had never married. They worked at the clothes factory in town where they had an apartment and came home on week-ends to the big house northeast across the creek from us where their elderly parents lived. We had often carried buckets of blackberries that we had picked over to sell to them, and now that I was doing the seed orders that my brother used to do I always went there because Mrs. Lawrence ordered a lot of seeds. I liked her and loved their big house and yard, but we had never visited very much with them. I noticed that Martha had quit work too and had sat down to rest after seating our guests.

Melinda, the older one, was talking as I slipped in and stood behind Mom's rocker. "Now that Mom is getting older we feel that she needs someone to help her with the work. We were wondering if we could hire Martha to work for her one day a week. It would be mowing the lawn, hoeing in the garden, dusting, etc. We'd be willing to pay a dollar for the day's work."

"I'm sorry," Mom said. "We'd be glad to help you out, but since I've just had this new baby, Martha has taken over here and I simply couldn't do without her now."

"Well, I can understand that," Melinda answered. "But we had hoped we could get Mom some help. If she sees a job to be done, she just up and does it, whether she's able or not."

"I could do it," I spoke up quickly. "I could work for her once a week for a dollar a day." The money sounded mighty appealing to me. Then as Martha and Mom both looked at me doubtfully, I went on defiantly. "You know I could do those kinds of things."

"I don't know about the mowing," Mom seemed hesitant. "You haven't done much of that, Ginny."

"But I did mow for Vivian a couple of times, and she wants me to do it the rest of the summer whenever Clifford can't." Vivian had a new baby boy too born in April so she needed some help now and then.

"That's right she did," put in Martha. "I'm sure she can do all right if you want to try her," she said to the Lawrence "girls."

"Sounds good to me," put in Edna, the younger of the two. "Could you start this Friday, Ginny?"

I glanced at Mom who nodded. "Yes, I could," I answered eagerly. "What time should I be there?"

"Let's make it eight o'clock," said Melinda. "Mom still gets up with the chickens and by eight o'clock she'll be rearing to go." Then turning to her sister she added, "We'd better go if we're going to get any cleaning done for Mom this afternoon." Then to Mom, "This is our afternoon off at the factory, and we always come out to do some heavy cleaning or whatever needs to be done."

Mom nodded for she already knew this as most everyone knew everything about everyone in a small community like ours. They admired the new baby, spoke to Janice and Alice who were hovering near, thanked me, and were gone.

"A job! A job! I have a job and will earn a whole dollar a day!" I twirled around and around in my cotton dress and bare feet while the rest of them laughed.

Martha didn't say anything then, but I later realized that she didn't think it was fair that I was to be paid, and she was working so hard and getting nothing. I promised myself that I'd somehow make it up to her. And for starters, I helped her finish the wash, cook supper, and then did the dishes myself so she could have some free time before getting all the little ones bathed before bed.

I was really excited about my new job and had trouble getting to sleep Thursday night. Mom had promised to waken me bright and early on Friday morning so I would have plenty of time to get there before eight o'clock. She had some scrambled eggs and hot biscuits waiting for me when I got to the kitchen as our bacon and ham from butchering was long since gone. After brushing my teeth, I kissed her good-by and took off across the north pasture. Mom with the baby in her arms stood on the back porch watching me go, "Do a good job and be careful with that mower," she called as I slid under the barbed wire fence then turned to wave.

At the walnut tree, I turned east and walked until I came to the fence that separated our land from Clifford's. I climbed the fence, a difficult feat when we had carried buckets of blackberries, and went on down to the creek. The water was shallow enough that I could cross easily. On the other side after scrambling up the bank, I was soon following the path up to their barn. Over in the field to my left, I saw Mr. Lawrence plowing his corn field with his team of big mules. I had hurried all the way so I was pretty sure that I wasn't late, but Mrs. Lawrence, a short elderly woman with her white hair pulled back in a tight bun at the back of her head and her blue eyes hid behind her wire framed glasses, was standing in the front yard shading her eyes with her hand and peering in my direction.

"Good morning, Mrs. Lawrence," I called. "I hope I'm not late," for I did want to make a good impression the first day on my new job.

"Why, it's nigh onto eight o'clock," she said in a snappy voice. "I thought maybe you weren't coming."

"But she said for me to be here at eight o'clock, and I hurried so that I wouldn't be late." My voice quivered and I was afraid that I might cry.

"Who said that?"

"Your daughter did when she hired me. That's what she said."

Then the old lady, she seemed so old to me, but was probably only in her sixties, smiled which made her face crinkle and her eyes look warm and she put a hand on my shoulder. "I was only teasing you, child. Don't get so upset. Come on for there's much to do. " And so began my first day on the new job working for Mrs. Lawrence for a dollar a day.

We decided that I should do the mowing first before the day got too hot. She had already wheeled out the push mower from the shed behind the house. Their yard was so big, more than three times as big as ours and much bigger than Vivian's, and part of it was up and down a sloping hill. I was afraid that it was much more than I had bargained for as I quickly grew very tired. But I was determined that I would not let it get me down so I tried to be cheerful and think of other things. After watching me for awhile, Mrs. Lawrence had gone back inside so I began to sing all the church songs that I could think of, my favorite being "At Calvary". I knew that I couldn't carry a tune very well, but out there pushing the lawn mower up and down the yard, I didn't think that it mattered. It was a long time later when I learned that Mrs. Lawrence always listened to me sing, and sometimes hummed along with me.

I had finished and was pushing the mower around to the shed when she came out of the screened in back porch which ran all along one side of the house. She carried a pitcher of lemonade and two glasses. I loved lemonade, but we seldom got to have it.

"Thought you might be thirsty," she said as she sat down on the top step and poured me a glass. I was amazed to find that it had ice in it.

"Oh, I am," I answered, "And I love lemonade. Thank you very much."

"Well good," she drawled. "I'm glad that I fixed something you like. I enjoy it too." She poured herself a glass and we drank happily while I sat on the bottom step resting my feet on the ground.

Then I asked her the question that I had to know the answer to, "Mrs. Lawrence, how did you get ice?" for I knew that like us they did not have electricity.

"That's a good question," she said. Then standing up she reached for my hand. "Come and I'll show you." I followed her through the screened porch and into the kitchen. There was the big cook range that burned wood, the pie safe, and table and chairs like in our kitchen with also the inevitable little table that held the water bucket, dipper, washpan and soap with a roller towel nearby, but there was also a big white refrigerator that stood right in the center of the long wall. She opened the top of it and showed me the trays of ice cubes. Then she took out one of the trays and showed me a frozen white mixture. "We even have homemade ice cream," she chucked, "And we'll have some for dinner."

My mouth watered at the thought, but I still had to know the answer. "But how does it work? You don't have electricity."

"It's a gas refrigerator," she explained. "It's run by gas and it's wonderful. Our children gave it to us for Christmas."

"That's great," I marveled. Then I added. "Someday I'll buy my mother one of those. Wouldn't she just love it?"

"I'm sure she would, but if we don't get to work, you'll never earn any money." She took my empty glass and put them both on the table. "Come, we need to do some hoeing in the garden before we start dinner."

Taking her sunbonnet from a hook on the wall, she led me out to her garden which was fenced in to keep the chickens out. I liked the hollyhocks, brillant with color, on each side of the garden gate. I had never liked hoeing, but with her helping me and talking to me as though I were a grown up, it wasn't too bad going up and down the rows, chopping out the weeds, and pulling the dirt up around the hills of cucumbers, pumpkins, and squash. I kept thinking about that homemade refrigerator frozen ice cream, and wondering how it would taste. Before long we were done with what she had planned to do, and she was pushing back her sunbonnet and looking up at the sun which was now high overhead and getting very hot.

"I think we had better go fix dinner, Ginny, for the old man will be in wanting his meal." She always called him the old man though I knew his name was Gorden, and I guessed they'd been married forever.

We hung the hoes on the garden fence and went inside where we carefully washed our hands in cold water and soap. She explained to me that she never fired up the stove in the summer time for she had an oil burning stove on the screened porch and she cooked out there. While I emptied the washpan outside after we had dried our hands on the roller towel, she lit the stove and began to fry some smoke cured ham that she had brought in from the smokehouse earlier. I was hungry and it smelled so good that I could harldy wait. I stood by the stove watching her eagerly.

"Well, who do we have here?" I turned at the sound of the voice and saw Mr. Lawrence coming in the side door. He was a tall old man with shaggy white hair and a long face, but his smile was warm and I didn't feel afraid.

He was dressed in dusty overalls and a long sleeved blue shirt.

"This is Ginny Haines, Joe and Pauline's girl," his wife answered. "Remember I told you she was going to come help me out?"

"Oh, yes, now I remember. How are you, Ginny?" he asked kindly.

"I'm fine, sir," I answered, and wanted to add, "And very hungry," but didn't.

He threw his strawhat on the floor and went into the kitchen to wash up. When he was done, I emptied the washpan and cleaned up his mess where he had sloshed water onto the floor with a rag Mrs. Lawrence had handed me after he went back out to the porch to lie down in the porch swing while she finished dinner. I hung the wet rag on a rack that she indicated wondering as I often did why men were so messy.

But she just smiled and shook her head.

"Now, Ginny, how about setting the table and putting some ice in our glasses so we can have some more lemonade?"

"Sure," I replied as I went back into the kitchen. I had noticed that she had a big pot of fresh green beans and new potatoes on the other burner of the oil stove and she was slicing a loaf of homemade yeast bread that was on a little table by the stove. If they ate like this all the time, I wished I could work for her every day, and just think of all the money I would make too.

The food was as delicious as I had imagined, and they kept urging me to eat more which I did. Then when we had cleared off the table, she dished us up some ice cream, which was as special as I had anticipated. When I thought all the wonderful surprises were over, she brought out a huge cookie jar that was filled to the brim with her own homemade honey nut cookies. I had never tasted anything so good!

Afterwards, Mr. Lawrence took a nap on the porch swing, which was the biggest one I had ever seen—he had made it so it would be long enough for him to stretch out on Mrs. Lawrence explained to me when I looked at it in awe—and Mrs. Lawrence rested in her rocker. I washed the dishes in a pan of cold water and homemade lye soap. I was glad that Mom always heated our water for dishes since washing them in cold water was truly icky and very difficult to get them clean. When she came in later to dry them and handed me back a plate saying, "Better lick this calf again," —her expression for "wash it again"— I wanted to say, "Get me some hot water," but I didn't.

She let me climb up on a tall stool and put the dishes away in the big cabinet built into the wall from floor to ceiling. Then it was time for me to dust. The two rooms across the front of the house were their bedroom and the living room with the dining room between the living room and the kitchen. The "girls"—and she always called them that—had their room behind the kitchen. She gave me a dustrag and told me to dust everything even the window sills.

I liked this house and pretended that it was mine while I worked. It was an old house and had heavy wooden doors even between the rooms, and they had great big keyholes. The windows were tall with strips of wood down between the panes. The floors that were not covered with carpets were wide oak boards that sometimes creaked when you walked. The furniture seemed magnificent compared to what we had at home, and I realized again that maybe Elizabeth was right when she talked about us being poor.

There were several little glass knickknacks on shelves or tables, I handled these carefully and fearfully. But as I started to put a little blue Dutch boy back on the table, it slipped from my fingers and fell to the floor. Even before I picked it up, I knew that it was broken, and I wanted to cry. My first thought was, I'll not say anything. I'll just put it back and maybe she won't notice it for a long time. She'll never know I did it. But I knew that wasn't true for she would know, and I knew that I would have trouble living with my conscience. It would be like a lie. So, bravely I took it in my hands and sought her out on the screened porch where she was doing some patching on her husband's overalls.

I stood before her a frightened little girl realizing that she might not want to have me work anymore, and even worse she might not pay me even for today after all my hard work. I held the broken Dutch boy behind me. My heart was beating wildly and I struggled to talk. She looked up at me and smiled.

"Are you done, Ginny?"

Not trusting myself to speak, I just shook my head.

"Well, what is it? Do you want something to drink, or do you just need to rest?"

I wished that she wouldn't be so kind. Trying to keep from crying, I brought the broken object out from behind my back and held it out to her. "I'm so sorry," I said all in a rush. "I accidently knocked it off and it broke. I didn't mean to, and I'll pay you for it. Just please let me keep working for you."

She took it in her hands and looked briefly at the broken arm. Then to my amazement, she laughed. "Don't worry about it, Ginny. It was broken before and I glued it." She pointed to the place where it had been glued. "See, there's the place. I'll just glue it again. I should have thrown it away, but kept it for sentimental reasons since one of my children gave it to me."

"Then you're not going to f-f-fire me?" I stammered.

"Of course not, child. I wouldn't have fired you even if you had broken something. But I do appreciate your coming to me with it. That was the honest thing to do. Now, run along and finish dusting, and when you're done, I have a special treat for you."

Feeling greatly relieved, I went back to my job glad that I had admitted what I had done instead of trying to hide it. When I went back to the screened porch, Mrs. Lawrence handed me a tall glass and bade me sit down and enjoy it. I found to my delight that it was some more of the homemade ice cream covered with Nehi orange soda. It was so good that I could hardly believe my good fortune.

"If you're not too tired," she said when I had finished, "I would like for you to rake up the chicken yard for me before you go home."

"No, I'm fine," I replied. "I'll be glad to do it. And thanks for the delicious drink."

As she took my glass from me, she reached out and patted my thick dark hair which I no longer wore in long curls. "I think you and I will get along just fine, Ginny." she said, "I like your style."

She came out to the chicken yard to show me what to do, and then ended up helping me rake and held the shovel while I swept the mess onto it with an old broom. While we worked, she told me a story about an old fox that had sneaked up from the creek one dark night and stole some of her hens. The next night when it came, the old man had taken his rifle out and shot at it, but he had missed. I was glad that the fox had not been hurt for I thought they were pretty animals.

Then before I knew it, I was washing my face and hands in the washpan in the kitchen, being careful not to spill any on the floor. She handed me my dollar, thanked me for a good day's work, I thanked her for the money, and was soon on my way.

I clutched the dollar tightly in my hand all the way home while I thought of all the various ways I would spend my hard earned money, but it ended up that I gave it to Mom the next day to help buy groceries since she didn't have enough for the necessities.

Chapter 12

Now I'm Eleven

I continued to work for Mrs. Lawrence all summer and even on Saturdays after school started until the weather got bad. I learned to love both of them as they showered their affection on me, I was pleased with all the money I earned, and I especially enjoyed all the delicious food and drinks, with a special love for her homemade honey nut cookies.

I had been so afraid that Mom would die when Ross was born that I still wanted to show my love and affection for her and my thankfulness to God for sparing her. For my prize for selling garden seed, I chose a whole set of dishes, off white with tiny colored flowers in the center, which I was able to do because I had a double order thanks to Mrs. Lawrence's generous one. I was so proud when the dishes came with Mr. Yates bringing them up to our house in his old Model A Ford instead of leaving them at the mailbox. I had kept it a secret from Mom so she was really surprised when I opened the box and showed her the lovely dishes. I thought they were the prettiest ones I had ever seen. There was even a meat platter which I envisioned piled high with crisp fried chicken.

"Oh, my," said Mom as she carefully examined each piece. "I've never had a whole set of dishes that matched before." As she hugged me, I felt like crying I was so happy.

Then as I helped Martha clean the house one day in hot July, I noticed that the curtains in our living room had holes in them and looked tattered and gray even though we had washed and ironed them. I decided then that I would use some of my precious earned money to buy Mom some new ones. When I had enough money, I took it down to Vivian's, my cousin who lived down the road and seemed almost like a big sister, and got her to order them out of the catalog for me so I could have another surprise for Mom. After they came, I decided that I had shown my thankfulness enough and could now save my money for some things I wanted, but many times that summer and fall I had to "loan" it to Mom to help with groceries. I did save enough to buy me and Martha some new tennis shoes for school. And Martha was so grateful that again I felt like crying.

I loved going down to Vivian's except when I was sent to borrow some baking powder, sugar, flour, or something else that Mom had run out of with no way to get more until they went to town on Saturday. Then I would talk about everything under the sun except the purpose of my visit, hemming and hawing, as the country people said, until finally the dreaded words would burst forth from my lips.

"Mom wanted to know if we could borrow some baking powder until Saturday," I'd finally say with a great deal of effort.

And Vivian would smile in her sweet way, nod her head, and give me more than I had asked for. She usually gave me a boughten cookie out of her cookie jar that always set on the shelf of her new cabinet.

I'll never borrow anything from anybody, or ask anyone to ever take me anywhere, I always told myself on the way home for we had to depend on them for transportation too.

Naomi had a baby girl born that summer soon after Ross was born so she would grow up with her uncle. I felt important being an aunt at ten years of age, and was happy when Naomi came back to Carmon to live with Larry's folks while he went overseas to fight in the war. She came down to visit us for a couple of weeks, and I loved having her there. I also loved taking care of her baby with her blonde hair and blue eyes and dimples in her cheeks, carrying her around, or rocking her to sleep. But I was sorry that Larry had gone away to war as it made Naomi sad, and she didn't laugh and sing like she used to do.

Joey and Elizabeth had both gotten married that spring, Elizabeth just after she graduated from high school. Thinking I was asleep one early spring morning, I overheard her telling Joey that she and Maurice, a young school teacher, were getting married. I told no one that I knew that secret until many years later. Everyone knew that Joey and Julia were getting married the month before. But now Joey had been drafted and gone away to train in the Air Force and Julia had gone along to live on the base. Maurice had a problem with his eyes so he was allowed to stay home and teach school. I missed Elizabeth a great deal, but they lived not far away and she often came to see us.

Martha and I continued all summer to go to 4-H meetings along with our friends at Hattie Austin's house. She lived on the other side of the creek so we had to go past Jones's Bluff where the man had been murdered. It was all right in the daytime, but when we had a night meeting, we would hurry past the bluff not saying a word so we wouldn't rouse up the ghost that we were sure lived there.

As I mentioned earlier, our project that summer was a Victory Garden because of the war. We had to care for our own little plot all summer, and when the vegetables were ready, we had to can them to show at our Achievement Night and to enter in the County Fair.

At our meetings each week, we had a business meeting then a program where we first recited the 4-H pledge:

I pledge my head to clearer thinking,
My heart to greater loyalty,
My hands to better service,

And my health to better living,
For my club, my community, and my country.

Then we sang some songs, had a talk about good health or safety, and a demonstration of how to do something about our project. Afterwards we played games and had refreshments. We all loved Hattie, who was a young married woman, but who seemed old to us, and we enjoyed being at her house.

One meeting day in July we had finished our program, and had just gone outside to play some games, when the sky grew very dark and threatening, and streaky lightning followed by tremendous claps of thunder indicated the coming storm.

"I think we had better go back inside," said Hattie.

"Or maybe to the fruit cellar," I suggested for I had inherited my mother's fear of storms, and could not keep my eyes off the clouds that grew dark in the west.

"Oh, Ginny," Martha said in an exasperated voice. "If Hattie thinks we should go to the cellar, she will tell us. You're not the one to make the decisions."

If I'd already bought her new shoes, I'd probably have taken them back, but since I hadn't I couldn't. So, I just looked up at Hattie hopefully, but she just smiled and put her arm around me.

"I think we'll be safe enough in the house, Ginny, but let's go now!"

Later I think we all wished that we'd gone to the cellar for it really stormed. Lightning streaked across the sky followed by thunder that shook the house, the wind blew so strongly that the tall trees in front of her house seemed to bend over double, then it hailed until the yard was covered with tiny balls of ice, and when the rain came it ran in sheets down the windows and soon the road looked like it was flooded. We didn't talk much, but just watched the storm and I prayed that we'd all be safe and that I wouldn't be so scared. When it began to slack off, we played some games inside and had refreshments. Betsy and Ginny had brought homemade peanut butter cookies and red Kool-Aid as it was their turn to furnish them.

We had just finished eating when we heard a, "Hello," from the back door, and when Hattie went to answer, it was our dad. When he came into the kitchen we looked up in surprise.

"What are you doing here?" Martha asked afraid that something had happened at home.

"I was afraid that the bridge would be flooded, and it is. So, I've come to walk you home."

We quickly cleared off the table and got ready to go. There were Betsy, Ginny, Ellen, Martha, and me so he had to make five trips across the flooded bridge floor holding our hands so we wouldn't fall, or step in the wrong place and perhaps go through a hole to the raging creek below. We had all heard the story about Daddy and his team of mules going into the creek after such a storm back when Naomi and Joey were little. One of the mules was drowned, and Daddy was all shook up, wet and cold, and might have drowned if neighbors hadn't come to help. We knew that was why he had come to see that we got home safely and we were grateful.

GINNY'S DREAM

At the end of the summer when our 4-H Club came to a close, we had a program called Achievement Night which we gave at night for the parents. We gave a program like we gave at our meetings, and then we did short plays and skits and songs and had a general good time. We usually did this at the church where Hattie and her two cousins attended because the deacons in our church at Hickory Grove were the uncles of us Haines, Haas, and Harper girls, and in our opinions they were mean, strict, unyielding old men who wouldn't let us have the program at our church for they considered it too frivolous to be held in the sacred house of God. Therefore, we got permission from the directors at our school, since Ellen's father was one of them, to have our program there.

It was probably a good thing that we didn't have it at the church that year because of the funny things that happened. It was a very hot night in mid August and we had a full house. Even with the windows open, it didn't help much and everyone was fanning.

We had a Mock Wedding with funny vows like: "Do you promise to sweep the floor, make the beds, and serve good hot biscuits every single morning?" for the bride dressed in an old lace curtain, and "Do you promise to plow the fields, hoe the taters, and milk the cow?" for the groom dressed in a long black coat and a tall hat made out of paper with some other foolishness thrown in.

Betsy Harper was the preacher and she got so tickled that she forgot her lines and they had to do it over and over until the whole house was howling with laughter.

Then Ginny Harper sang a solo, "The Barefoot Boy with Shoes on Stood Sitting on the Grass", that went on and on with that kind of nonsense.

Now, it was time for some serious stuff and Ellen went on stage to do a demonstration of how to make cornbread as last year our project had been quick breads, and Hattie figured that it would be easier to make cornbread, even though every woman in the audience probably made it every day to eat for supper with glasses of cold milk, than it would be to try to can something from our gardens. Ellen was to read her recipe, then carefully tell what she was doing step by step as she made the cornbread.

"First, you add a cup of cornmeal," Ellen said in her strongest loudest voice.

Since she didn't go on, the rest of us waiting in the cloakroom peered through the door, and quickly saw the problem. Ellen was looking frantically all over the table and then back at us with pleading eyes. There was no bag of cornmeal on the table. She had somehow forgotten to bring it.

"First, you add a cup of cornmeal," she repeated for the second time, and we could see that she was getting desperate.

Suddenly, an inspiration hit me. I grabbed up a sack of sand sitting in the cloakroom that we had used for another project of putting out a fire, and rushed on stage with it. Ellen flashed me a grateful smile, repeated for the third time, "First, you add a cup of cornmeal," and as calmly as though she were an actress on stage, dipped her cup into the bag of sand and poured it into the bowl.

Then went on with the rest of the ingredients. Since she had no way to bake it then, no one knew that she had made sand-bread instead of cornbread, and most of them never did find out.

It was now time for our grand finale. We were going to do the play about Clementine. Hattie sang the song while we acted it out. Martha was the old miner and Ellen was another miner. They were dressed in some of their dads' old overalls and shirts and hats with their hair pulled up under them. The other girls were the ducklings who squatted down holding their ankles while they waddled across the stage. Thrill of all thrills! I was Clementine! I was so proud and so wanted it to turn out right.

Two or three times I drove the ducklings across the stage, around through the cloakroom, and back across the stage. Then we came to the part of the song where she stumps her toe and falls into the foaming brine. I was backstage when Hattie sang that part so the ducklings dumped a bucket of water on me to drown me. Then the miners carried me onstage, laid me down, and covered me with a sheet for I was now dead. But they went backstage and forgot that they were to come carry me off again for we had no curtains.

I lay there waiting and waiting for what seemed like an eternity, but was really only a few minutes. Then I began to whisper loudly, "You're supposed to come and get me." Finally, I could stand it no longer, and to the delight of the audience, I, a dead person, stood up, picked up my sheet, and left the stage. They claimed that they just forgot to come back and get me, but I really believed that they did it on purpose because they were jealous that I got to be Clementine. Whatever the reason, it's probably a good thing that we didn't have that particular program at the church.

The next week we took some of our vegetables, fresh and canned to the county fair, which they always claimed was bigger and better every year. I got a red ribbon for my can of beets which looked shiny and red through the glass jar, and I was pleased with that. But I think I got more delight out of seeing some of Mrs. Lawrence's quilts hanging on a bar with blue ribbons on each of them, and a plate of her wonderful honey nut cookies placed among the bakery goods and beautifully adorned with another blue ribbon. For I felt that if anyone deserved them, she did.

The following Sunday was what we called "The All Day Dinner" at church though we really didn't eat all day, but we always had enough food that we could have if our bodies could have taken it. It was a wonderful day and one that we children always looked forward to with much delight. Vivian and Clifford always came to this, even though they didn't come to church all the time, so Mom, Daddy, and the little ones rode with them while the rest of us walked like we always did.

It started as usual with Sunday School at 10:00. There were two classes for the younger ones in the basement of the church. I was in the one for third through sixth graders, but I longed to move up to the little room behind the sanctuary where the seventh through high schoolers were taught by Randall Sims. He was Mom's cousin's husband, and everyone thought he was the best Sunday School teacher in the world. But the main reason that I wanted to be in that class was because the other Ginny had got to move up as well as Martha and Ellen already being there.

Randall was also Sunday School superintendent from as far back as I could remember. He also led the singing while Vivian played the piano. We always sang three hymns, standing on the last one for the responsive reading of the Sunday School lesson printed on a leaflet which the secretary passed out while we sang. Then someone led in prayer and we were dismissed to our classes. All the adults stayed in the sanctuary with Ginny's elderly uncle who taught them for years. Our teacher was his wife, a gentle, sweet, kind person who I am sure was a good Christian, but her slip always showed and her glasses were always falling down over her nose, and I had a tendency to pay attention to those things instead of the lesson. How I longed to go upstairs to the Young People's class!

But back to the All Day Dinner. After Sunday School, we had preaching once a month, and we always had our dinner on that Sunday in August. Several more people came in for church on that particular day. Some of them were people who used to live in our community and had moved away. I looked at the women in their lovely flowered dresses and big hats, high heeled shoes and stockings, and I vowed that someday when I was rich and famous, I would dress like that and come back to those dinners.

GINNY'S DREAM

Our preacher was an elderly man who preached at three other little country churches. He farmed in between and didn't have much education, but he'd had a call from God to preach, and he could really shout though I was never too sure that I understood what he was saying. Maybe I didn't listen too good. But on this day, he always outdid himself with so many visitors present. I thought he would never stop for I was so anxious for that long looked for dinner on the church lawn under the tall hickory nut trees.

Finally, he was through. The last song and prayer were done, and we were free. After racing with Ginny through the cemetery where our ancestors were buried, down to the outdoor toilet, we washed out hands under the pump, and then joined the other children to stare hopefully at the long tables covered with white tablecloths. Another long prayer was said, they removed the cloths, put spoons in the dishes and forks on the platters of crispy fried chicken or cured ham, and we could begin.

There were homemade dumplings, green beans, all kinds of potatoes from mashed to little new ones cooked with fresh green peas to potato salad, ripe tomatoes, baked corn and corn on the cob, every vegetable you could think of plus all kinds of pickles and relishes. Then the desserts were something else again -- pies of all kinds, cake (chocolate, white, angel food, or pink frosted), cookies, fruit, and barrels of lemonade. I thought this must be what Heaven was like with this much good food -- so much you couldn't eat it all. That was the only trouble.

I always wished I could take a plateful home to eat tomorrow.

In the afternoon, we had a quartet of men who usually sang Stamps Baxter music. And then one or two preachers. Maybe we should have called it All Day Preaching instead of All Day Dinners. This particular afternoon we kids all got tickled at Bill and Kevin Matthews' mother who sat on the front pew behind the piano so she could fan the piano player with the huge fan that she always carried, almost falling off her seat in the process. It didn't help that she was, as we unkindly called her, "big and fat." When we finally got home, we were amazed to find that we were hungry again and eager to dig out the food that Mom had left over in her basket.

The twenty-fifth of August is my birthday, and that year on August 25, 1942, I was eleven years old. One minute it seemed like I was growing up entirely too fast, and the next it seemed that I would never reach the age where I could do the things that Martha and Ellen did, or go the places they went. They seemed so grownup and I felt that I had lost my childhood playmates as indeed I had.

Mom seldom could afford to buy us birthday presents, but she always made a special dinner for the birthday person, and we could choose what we wanted. I was glad that mine came in August for the things I loved the very best, well, almost the very best, were available then. I always wanted the same things so when Mom asked the night before what I would like for my birthday dinner, before I could answer Martha spoke up.

"Fried chicken, green beans, mashed potatoes, sliced tomatoes, roasting ears and—"

"And chocolate cake," Janice, who was now six, interrupted, "With chocolate icing."

"Cake," repeated little Alice. "Cake, cake, cake." She followed Janice around everywhere repeating all she said and did. Her red hair lay in little ringlets all over her head, and her eyes were big and brown like Naomi's.

Janice tossed her long blonde braids while her gray eyes snapped. "Oh, Alice, don't say everything I do."

Mom, who was sitting in the big rocker on the back porch while she nursed the baby, just laughed. "I think they have your number, Ginny," she said as she gazed at all of us fondly.

"Well, she always wants the same dumb things," insisted Martha. "I like to try new and different things."

Now, it was our turn to laugh at her for we never had new or different things. It was always the same—winter and summer, summer and winter.

"But those are the things I love," I argued. Then turning to Mom, I asked, "Can we have that for my birthday dinner, Mom?"

"Yes, if you'll go to the cornfield down by the creek in the morning to pick the green beans and the roasting ears." We always called corn on the cob roasting ears.

Next morning I went to the creek early before the sun got too hot. I picked a big bucket of green beans from the vines that grew up the sides of the cornstalks. Then I carefully chose a dozen ears of corn from the stalks that reached up higher than my head, testing each one to see if it still had milk in the kernels of corn by sticking my finger nail in each ear. Then I waded in the cold water of the creek to cool off before loading my harvest on our little red wagon to pull back up the road to our house.

When I got there, Mom was out behind the smokehouse dipping two big roosters into a bucket of boiling water to make their feathers easier to pluck off. I was glad that Daddy had wrung their heads off before I got back because much as I loved fried chicken I didn't like the killing process. She looked up with a smile at what I had brought.

"Your daddy is waiting out under the pear tree to help you string and snap the beans and shuck the corn," she said as she began to pluck the first chicken.

I pulled the wagon out to the pear tree where indeed Daddy was waiting. He sat in an old rocker dressed as usual in his faded overalls and long sleeved blue shirt. His straw hat perched on the top of his bald head. Two big pans awaited the vegetables at his feet. Janice and Alice played with their dolls in the grass nearby and baby Ross lay on a pallet close to the rocker.

"Here are the beans and corn," I said as I pulled the wagon close to his chair.

"Well, looks like you got enough for an army," he laughed. "Guess we had better get to work on them." He took a handful of the long green beans from the bucket and put them on the newspaper in his lap. He began to snip off the ends and break the beans in small pieces then throw them into the pan.

"I'll help you as soon as I go get a drink of water and wash my face," I said as I turned for the kitchen. As I climbed up on the little porch that ran between the smokehouse and the kitchen, he called to me.

"Happy birthday, Ginny," and I smiled to myself for I wondered if anyone had remembered.

In the hot kitchen with a fire going in the wood stove as usual, Martha was making my chocolate cake so I knew she had remembered too. I drank a dipper full of water from the water bucket on the little table then washed my face and hands in the water in the wash pan. Then I went to help prepare the vegetables.

When Naomi started working, she always got me presents for my birthday. But now she was married and had a baby so I didn't expect any. So, I was greatly surprised when Janice went to the mailbox and came back with a card for me from Naomi, and taped inside were two shiny quarters. She hadn't forgotten after all I thought as happiness swept over me. Then I had another surprise which Mom knew about all along. While she was frying the chicken and the beans and corn were boiling away on the hot cookstove, a car pulled in the drive and there were Elizabeth and Maurice come to eat my birthday dinner with me. I was delighted and even more so when she put some store bought candles on my cake, lit them, and led everyone in singing "Happy Birthday" to me. Then she gave me a small brightly wrapped present and inside were two blue barrettes for my hair. Martha had helped the little girls to make me a card and Mom had fixed my special dinner. I felt that I was very lucky indeed.

Elizabeth even insisted on helping Martha do the dishes and I was told that I could go do whatever I wanted. Whenever I had that opportunity, I fled to the hayloft with a pad of paper and a pencil to work on my book that I was someday going to write.

When I came back to the house, Elizabeth was helping Daddy peel peaches out in the yard while Maurice helped Martha pick them in the orchard, and Mom canned them in the hot kitchen. It might be my birthday, but it was a work day as usual for everyone else.

I slipped up to the heavy crock that set on the grass by Daddy's chair where he was putting big halves of peaches, put my hand inside, snatched up two big halves and popped them one after another into my mouth. Elizabeth saw me and laughed. "You better stop that, Ginny, or Mom will get you, birthday girl or not." We knew that gentle patient Daddy wouldn't say anything, but Mom, who always had to think of food for the long cold winters, took a different approach. Feeling tired of doing nothing, I sauntered over to the orchard to help pick peaches.

I thought my day had been perfect, but I had yet another surprise. Just about dark a car pulled in the drive and Hattie Austin got out. I ran out to greet her and she said to me, "Happy Birthday, Ginny." I guessed she knew from my 4-H records. Then she added, "I have some pretty blue and white checked material left over from my kitchen curtains, and I thought you might like to have a new dress for school. Let's go ask your mother if you can come up tomorrow so I can measure and fit you."

GINNY'S DREAM

When I said my prayers that night, I just said, "Thank you, God," over and over for my wonderful eleventh birthday. Surely no one anywhere had ever had such a day!

Chapter 13

The Gralleys, the Goat, and the Gloves

When school started the next week, I was in sixth grade. It seemed strange that Ginny and I were now the oldest girls in school since Martha and Ellen had gone on to high school. They caught the bus at our school so sometimes if I got ready in time, I walked with them. But Janice was in first grade that year and I usually had to wait for her.

We had another new teacher. This one was named Mr. Turley. He was old and bald and very strict. We thought at first that none of us would like him, and we never did like him as much as we had the others particularly Mr. Birkey. One thing that he did made me very angry, and that was to cater to silly little Milly Jean just because her father was one of the school directors.

He didn't cater to Victor and Burt, or the other children whose fathers were directors, but always "darling little Milly Jean" had to have her way. This strengthened my determination to be a teacher when I grew up and not to favor the directors' children.

Since I was one of the older girls, I finally got to realize my dream of listening to the little ones read, and help them with their math and printing. This I thoroughly enjoyed, and always hurried through my assignments so that I could "teach." I think I helped Janice and Burt more than the teacher did.

A new family came to our school that year, and poor as most of us were, this family was socially inferior to the rest of us. We all probably realized that it was the parents' fault that the children came to school so dirty and had such disgusting manners, but that didn't keep us from being mean and cruel to them.

There were three of them — Daisy in fifth grade, Molly in third and little despicable Georgie in first. Whenever he came outside, someone was sure to sing:

Georgie Porgie Pudding and Pie,
Kissed the girls and made them cry.

And it made us sick at our stomachs to even think about him kissing any of us.

Since we were farm kids, we all got dirty doing the chores and things that we had to do, but we wore old clothes for that and school clothes for school. Some of us, particularly the boys, got dirty playing ball or other games at school, but we didn't come to school that way. We were all clean when the day started, all that is except the Gralley children—they were dirty all the time. Their clothes were filthy, their faces and hands were always dirty and Georgie always had snot running out of his nose and down on his lip, (that's why I decided that I could never eat pumpkin pie again after seeing him eat a piece one day in that condition), and their hair was matted and dirty, looking like it had lice, whether or not it did. All of this tended to make us mean and unkind, singing little ditties about them, and refusing to let them join our games or groups. The surprising thing was that the teacher didn't do much to try to get us to change our minds. I guess he couldn't abide them either.

Even the other Ginny, who was usually so kind and sweet, didn't want to play with them, or even have them near us. If a person doesn't take a bath for a long time and wears dirty clothes all the time, pretty soon that person begins to smell pretty badly. We couldn't understand how anyone could stand to be so dirty. I got to change my few school dresses whenever I wanted, or if they got dirty, but Ginny's mother made her wear the same dress every day for a week before changing so she had to be very careful to keep it clean. My new blue and white checked dress that Hattie had made me I had worn on the first day, but then kept it for special occasions and church.

One sunny fall day when Ginny and I had raced out to the swings to beat the smaller girls so we could swing while we ate our lunches, mine being fried green tomatoes on biscuits, apples picked up off the ground, and some late grapes off Vivian's vines, we had to make a decision. We had just reached the swings, and started to eat when who should come over but dirty Daisy. There was an empty swing as the other girls had settled for a grassy spot under the tall hickory nut tree, and most of the boys were eating by the ball diamond so they could begin to play as soon as they had swallowed the last bite. Sometimes Victor, Ellen's brother, and Bill Matthews started throwing the softball back and forth even while they were still eating. We had real good health habits about eating in those days.

"Can I sit here?" asked Daisy indicating the empty swing.

I looked at Ginny in despair, but she answered calmly. "You can if you want to, but I would advise you not to."

"And why not?" Daisy demanded still standing there in her dirty dress holding a brown paper bag in her hand.

"Because if you swing and eat at the same time you will get very sick. You may even have to go to the hospital," Ginny told her.

In a dejected way, Daisy turned away, but then turned back to ask defiantly, "Then why doesn't it make you two sick?"

I looked at Ginny wondering what her answer was going to be, but she stayed as calm as before. "We took shots for it, but we took them a long time ago and you can't even get them now."

Daisy left us going over to Molly who had already been refused permission to join the other girls. They sat on the porch steps looking at us, and probably wondering why they were being treated so. Georgie just wandered around the playground annoying everyone he came near.

I was still staring at Ginny in astonishment. "Ginny, you lied to that girl. Whatever were you thinking of?" I wondered if God would send lightning from Heaven to strike her off the swing.

Ginny seemed less sure now that Daisy was gone, but she shrugged her shoulders and said, "Well, I got rid of her didn't I?"

"Yes, you did," I answered, but somehow I had trouble getting my food to go down and my stomach felt a little queasy. But Daisy didn't ask to join us in the swings anymore.

Jack Austin, who had helped us conquer the bee tree, had a little sister named Nancy and she was in fifth grade this year. She had always played ball with her older brothers and was very good. So, Mr. Turley put her on the softball team that fall, and then he asked Ginny and me to play. Ginny declined, but I decided to try it, and surprised everyone by being so good that I ended up playing first base. I guess all those ball games that we had played at home using a stick for a bat and a rubber ball had paid off after all. I loved it and began to spend most of my time practicing. Ginny and I still ate lunch together, but then she watched and played with the little ones while I played ball. Daisy and Milly still wandered around by themselves like little lost waifs. Ginny's brother Rex, who was my age, but still in fifth grade, liked me and said that he was my boyfriend. I liked this in a secret sort of way, and felt that he would protect me if any of the others caused trouble.

When we went to other schools to play games, Ginny usually stayed with the little kids that didn't go, although sometimes a parent or two would come in their cars or trucks and take everyone. One afternoon I had a terrible headache and didn't feel like playing ball so I stayed at school with her too.

They hadn't been gone too long when the sky became very dark and the wind began to blow. I felt the familiar feeling of fear that I always got when a storm approached, and I wished that I had gone with them anyway.

"What are we going to do?" I whispered to Ginny.

"We'll just go on with classes," she whispered back, "And maybe none of them will get too scared." She knew how frightened I was of storms, but chose to ignore it.

We went on working with the little children and ignoring the Gralley children as usual. Then suddenly there was a bright steak of lightning and a tremendous crash of thunder that seemed to shake the building and then the lights went off. It was terribly dark even though it was the middle of the afternoon. The wind howled and the lightning and thunder continued. Then it began to rain in torrents as it ran down the windows. We huddled together in a little group, too frightened to even be concerned when the dirty children crowded close to us.

When the fury of the storm began to abate, we gathered at the windows to look out. And suddenly a horse dashed past the window. It was Bill Matthews's big black horse that he rode to school each day and tied to a tree at the far end of the schoolyard. Staring out through the rain soaked windows, we could see that the branch that it had been tied to had been broken in the storm and it was on its way home.

Silently I thanked God that we had all been spared, and then looking at Daisy and her little brother and sister, standing apart again. I asked Him to forgive Ginny and me for being so mean to them.

But when the sun shines, you sometimes forget those prayers and promises. It was only the next week when we persuaded Mr. Turley to take us girls, (there were fewer girls than boys and we knew we'd all fit in his car) to the big overhead bridge that stretched high above the railroad track to see a troop train go by. We had been assigned a report about trains, and we convinced him that this would help us on our assignment and we could even do a picture of the train.

When Ginny and I, as the oldest girls, went to ask him, he stopped what he was doing and ran his hands across his bald head. Then he looked at us over his glasses. "All of the girls?" he asked.

"Sure," I answered. "There are only eight girls and we can all fit in your car."

"Are you including Daisy and Molly?"

"Well, yes," said Ginny. "We figured that we had to."

"I suppose so," he agreed. Then he suggested something that I thought I would never hear a teacher say. "If you can persuade them to ride in the trunk of the car, we can go. But they're so dirty I really don't want them to ride in my car. You do understand, don't you?"

Of course, we understood, but nevertheless we stood there with our mouths open unable to speak. Even though we had treated them in an unspeakable way, we couldn't imagine a teacher doing such a thing. But we wanted to go, and if that were the only way, we would somehow arrange it. So, we went outside to the playground and walked over to Daisy and Molly, who as usual were standing alone under a tree, as though we talked to them every day.

"Hi, girls," I said in a friendly way as they looked at me in surprise. "We have persuaded Mr. Turley to take us girls to the overhead bridge tomorrow to see the troop train go by. You see, we thought it might help us with our report on trains."

"Yes?" Daisy looked at us questioningly as she pushed her lank dark hair back with her dirty fingers. "What's that got to do with us?"

"Yeah, what's that got to do with us?" repeated Molly looking at us with her dull blue eyes from under her long blonde bangs.

"Well, you have been chosen for the special honor of riding in the trunk of the teacher's car." I said. "You see, we all can't fit up front so two people have to ride in the trunk. Ginny and I wanted to, but Mr. Turley said that since you two were the newest girls at school that you should get that privilege. Okay?"

Ginny stared at me surprised that I was telling such a lie. But as no lightning came from Heaven, or I wasn't struck dumb, I guess she figured that it was all right. We both looked at the two outcast girls.

"With the lid shut?" asked Daisy as though she didn't like the idea.

"Oh, no," I put in quickly. "He'll leave it open and drive real slow. You'll have the best seat in the house."

"Sure, we'll do it," said Molly answering for both of them. Daisy didn't say anything, but a slow smile spread across her face. I guess it was better to be accepted in this way than not at all.

We went on our trip the next afternoon with the Gralley sisters thinking they were the lucky ones instead of the outcasts that they really were, and none of us bothered to tell our mothers about the incident for they would certainly have objected to our treatment and Mr. Turley's treatment of those girls just because they were dirty. If the girls thought that this would change our treatment of them at school, they were mistaken for we continued to treat them in the same old unkind unyielding way. But sometimes Ginny and I did feel pangs of remorse that we had lied to them and treated so badly just because they were dirty and disgusting looking. We especially felt badly after seeing the parents when they dropped them off one morning for they were dirty too and their clothes were so bad they looked like they stuck to them.

"Maybe we've been too harsh about them," said Ginny. "If our mother was that dirty, maybe we'd be dirty too."

"No way," I answered indignantly. "As old as they are, especially Daisy, they could clean themselves up and even wash their own clothes. You know we both help with the washing."

"That's true," she agreed. "But I guess they just don't have any incentive."

"Well, being clean should be their incentive," I said. "My mother always says that we may be poor, but we always have plenty of water and soap and there is no excuse for being dirty."

That seemed to salve our conscience for a long time. And I think we were all glad, even the teacher, when in the early spring, they suddenly moved away as quietly as they had come.

School was out, and I was faced with a new problem. Instead of getting better, Nanny, the goat, had continued to get worse. She hadn't gotten too big, but was stronger and, if possible, more stubborn than ever. She absolutely refused to stay in the pigpen, jumping over the fence as soon as I put her in there. It had become a real struggle to drag her to the barn whenever someone came in a car for she fought us every step of the way. Sometimes, I just didn't take her and prayed instead that she wouldn't climb on top of their cars, but she always did. And Janice, who was now seven, still screamed in fear that Nanny would fall off and get hurt though she never did. She still climbed up on top of the cistern top too and Janice still screamed about that. Baby Ross who was now a year old was crawling around, or pulling himself up. If we put him out in the yard when she was out, she refused to leave him alone and usually ended up knocking him over, or butting him gently with her head. It didn't really hurt him, but it scared him and made him cry. Alice, who was now four, was afraid of the goat and refused to even go outside when Nanny was around. So, it had become a real problem.

One June afternoon it seemed that everything had gone wrong concerning Nanny — Alice had cried because she was afraid to go out, Ross had cried because he'd been pushed down while holding onto a chair to walk around it, and Janice had screamed and cried after Nanny climbed proudly on top of Aunt Marie's car and tried to eat the leaves off the maple tree overhead—I'd had a terrible time getting her down, afraid all the time that she'd scratch Uncle Leonard's car, and he'd be mad and never take me anywhere ever again. I kept hoping that I could get her off the car before Aunt Marie came out of the house and saw her. And despite all the noise that Janice was making, I finally succeeded and dragged her off to the barn.

After Aunt Marie left, Mom called me into the kitchen. "Ginny," she said. "Something has to be done about that goat."

"I'm sorry, Mom, that I didn't put her in the barn when Aunt Marie came. Next time I will try to remember."

"It isn't just that, Ginny. It's all the things that she does. We can't have her bothering the little ones, and Janice's screaming about that stupid goat has got to stop."

"Oh, Janice acts so silly," I said scornfully. "I don't think she really cares about the goat. I think she just wants attention."

"Well, whatever." Mom rubbed her forehead as though it ached and pushed her dark reddish hair away from her eyes. "Whatever the reason it's got to stop. I simply cannot put up with it any longer and that's final."

I really had good intentions and promised myself that I would watch her closely, but no sooner had I turned her out the next morning for her exercise then she ran to the house, first to climb on the cistern where the top had been left up. She teetered unsteadily on the edge with me frightened that she would fall in before I could reach her. As I stretched out my hands for her neck, she jumped and fortunately landed on the ground. Before I could catch her, she had jumped upon the back porch and almost got in the screen door when Martha opened it to bring out some dish water to dump.

"Oh, Ginny, for heaven's sake, do something with this dumb goat," Martha yelled as water splashed over her clean dress. Though the goat partly belonged to her too after our cattle drive day, she had never liked it like I had and had by now become thoroughly disgusted with it.

"I'm trying. I'm trying," I said, and snatching at Nanny's collar again was finally sucessful in grabbing it, and yanking her off the porch. Going down the path to the barn, I was wondering what to do with her when I suddenly spied the cows peacefully grazing out in the pasture. "That's what I'll do," I said to myself. "I'll put her out in the pasture with the cows."

I did and to the amazement of all of us, she stayed there for several days. Then one morning she discovered that she could crawl under the barbed wire fence with just a few scratches on her back and out she came again. This time she sealed her doom by eating some of my mother's precious rose bushes. We always teased our mother about loving her flowers more than she did her kids, and when it came to roses, maybe she did. Anyway, it was definitely the straw that broke the camel's back!

"Ginny, come here this very instant," when Mom yelled like that I knew that she was really angry so I closed the book that I had been reading, jumped down from my perch in the old pear tree on the west side of the house, and ran to the front yard. Mom was standing by the front window looking down at her prize pink rosebush that was now nothing but some scrubby roots and a few thorny stems. She looked angry enough to bite nails and there were tears in her eyes. Nanny stood a few feet away happily eating the last of the leaves while a shattered pink rose or two lay at her feet.

"Oh, Mom, I'm so sorry," I blurted out as I took in the scene.

"It's not just this one," said my mother who was usually so calm. "Look over there." And sure enough the red rosebush on the other side of the porch was gone too.

"Bad Nanny," I shouted as I approached my pet with my hand raised to strike her, but Mom's voice halted it in midair.

"No, Ginny," she said in a strange way. "Being sorry is not good enough, and hitting that animal won't do any good. Now, is the time! She has to go!"

"Go? Go where?" I asked in astonishment. "Where would she go?"

"Back to your Uncle Albert where she should have stayed in the first place. Now, go get a rope from the barn and take her there before I lose my mind."

"But what will he do with her?" I asked.

"He'll put her in the pasture with his cows," Mom answered, and before I could raise another protest she added, "He has an electric fence so she'll stay there. Now, go quickly before I do something that I may always regret." She bent over her rosebush and I was sure that she was crying. I felt really badly as I started to the barn for the rope.

When I came back through the yard leading Nanny with the rope, she was waiting for me with Janice at her side. "Janice wants to go with you," she said, and after what had happened I didn't dare protest. But I did question.

"How do you know Uncle Albert will take her back?"

"Because when I complained to him about giving her to you in the first place, he said that anytime she became too much for me I could send her back. Now, is the time. Go!"

So, with Janice walking along beside me talking brightly about how we wouldn't have to worry about Nanny getting hurt anymore, and with my heart as heavy as lead because I was giving up my pet, we walked up the north road, past Jones's Bluff, across the creek bridge, past our cornfield and on up to his house. Uncle Albert was in the barnlot and he laughed when he saw us coming.

"Your mom's had enough?" he chuckled.

"Yes, Uncle Albert, she said that we had to bring Nanny back," I said softly. And I handed him the rope, took Janice's hand, and turned quickly away before I cried.

He did put her in his pasture for I sometimes saw her when we passed his house, but suddenly she was no longer there, and I never knew if he sold her, butchered her, or she somehow managed to escape, but I always hoped for the latter.

Old Mervin, who lived down by our creek where Ellen and I had stolen the watermelon four summers ago, had remarried. Her name was Lucinda Corn, and she was as eccentric as her name. We kids even thought that maybe she was a witch, and once we had hidden outside her cabin's kitchen window to see if she were doing any witchery, but she caught us and that ended that. Whenever they went anywhere in their old Model A Ford, she always rode behind Mervin, and when questioned, answered, "If that old fool hits anything, I am safer back here."

She had a grown son named Simon who lived with them. He was even stranger than her, or so we thought, for he worked little, talked to himself, and wandered the fields and bluffs like a child. Sometimes he came to our house on Saturday night to listen to the Grand Ole Opry on the radio. Or, that is what we thought that's what he came for because he said not a word to anyone except a mumbled, "Hello," when he came and Daddy greeted him with, "Hello, Simon, how are you tonight?"

He would take off his hat, sit on the horsehair couch that we had inherited from Grandpa Rensack, and which we all thought was terribly uncomfortable, close his eyes and listen. When the Grand Ole Opry was over, he would get up, put on his hat, and leave, all without saying a word.

So, we were all greatly surprised when one night that summer, when he got up to leave, he turned to my father, and said, "Joe, did you ever talk to an owl?"

Daddy looked at him in surprise. "No, I don't reckon I ever did, Simon."

"I did," said Simon. "I did just the other night when I was walking through the woods."

"You did what?"

"I talked to an owl. This old owl said, "Who, who, who?" And I stopped right there in the woods in the dead of night and I said, 'I'm Simon Corn. Who are you?' Yes, sir, I talked to that old owl, but he never answered me a thing." And then he put on his hat, and walked out our front door without saying another thing.

Needless to say, we all burst into laughter, even Mom and Daddy, as soon as the door had closed behind him. It was hard to not laugh when he came the next Saturday night, but Mom had threatened us beforehand so we were quiet. In all the times that he came after that, he never said another word. I supposed that he'd had one story to tell and he'd told it.

Lucinda came often to see my mother, and my mother, who was kind to everyone, treated her in the kindest manner possible, stopping her work to sit and visit, offering her a cup of coffee, or a glass of cold water from the well, or a piece of freshly baked pie or cake. Lucinda was always dressed in outlandish clothes with purple being her favorite color. Even on the hottest summer days, she wore long sleeved dresses that reached nearly to her ankles with stockings and shoes, had on some kind of wild creation of a hat, and she always wore gloves, but they were always old and the fingers were always out. I couldn't take my eyes off those gloves.

One afternoon I was ironing with the irons that had to be heated on the stove then picked up with a clasp handle to hold while you ironed. The main trouble was that they cooled off so quickly that you spent half your time changing irons. A fire was going in the range to heat the irons so it was very hot in the kitchen even though the windows and door were open. Mom, who was just finishing up canning some blackberries that Martha and I had picked that morning, and I were both wearing simple cotton dresses and we both were barefooted. When a knock sounded at the front door, Mom went through to answer and came back with Lucinda in tow. As usual, she was in her full ensemble complete with fingerless gloves. When Mom offered her some fresh blackberry cobbler, I thought she would at least remove her gloves, but she didn't. How she endured the heat of that kitchen in that getup, I'll never know!

While I ironed, I listened to them talk.

"Pauline," she said to my mother. "I am dreadful afraid of storms. When I see a cloud darken up in the west, I nearly die with fright."

"I can certainly sympathize with that," said Mom. "I used to feel exactly the same way."

I stopped ironing and looked at my mother in surprise for I thought she was still very much afraid of storms. But when she went on, I realized what she was doing.

"I find that my faith and trust in God help me through all of the storms of life, even the ones that come out of the clouds. Why don't you start coming to our church, Lucinda? I believe that God could help you too."

"Oh, I couldn't do that!" she exclaimed. "The old fool doesn't believe in God or the church and he'd never let me go."

"Then why don't you come over here when it storms and we'll all sit on the featherbeds together?"

"You mean you wouldn't care if I did that?" she asked in surprise.

"Of course not," my mother answered, and I felt a pang of remorse about the terrible way we had treated the Gralleys for I knew that my mother would have been kind and helpful even though they were dirty.

The rest of that summer and the next whenever a dark cloud appeared in the west, we would see Lucinda, all dressed up in her finery including the gloves without fingers, coming quickly up the road to stay with us until the storm was over.

Chapter 14

Decisions

W hen school started that fall, there were two important differences. For the first time we had a woman teacher, and for the first time since I had been in second grade, I was not in a class by myself. Mrs. Stillmore was the wife of the County Superintendent of schools, and she didn't want to teach both seventh and eighth grades so she moved me up to eighth grade with Ginny and Bill Matthews. I was delighted to be with Ginny, and all year long I hoped that Mrs. Stillmore would let me go on to high school the next year with her instead of staying there to do seventh grade. But all along I knew that she wouldn't and she didn't. "Rules are rules," she was fond of saying. Another one of her sayings was, "It takes more muscles to frown than it does to smile, so why work so hard?"

GINNY'S DREAM

Mrs. Stillmore was a large woman with very black hair and snapping dark eyes. She wore pretty dresses and she smiled often, but she was very strict with all of us. She didn't practice ball or track with us, but just let us do it on our own so she didn't "waste" school time on such trivial things. But she read to us every afternoon after lunch, and this soon became my favorite time of day. I had always loved to read, but it became more intensified that year as I felt myself become a part of every book she read. And as I listened to stories about different parts of our big country and places way across the ocean, I vowed to myself to someday travel to all those places to see them for myself.

Now, more than ever I wanted to become a writer, and I spent more and more time in the hayloft, or perched up in the pear tree, or in a chair behind the heating stove in the wintertime always writing in my little notebook. Since the war was still raging in Europe, I decided to write a story about a German war spy. I didn't realize that I would be better off writing about something that I knew a lot about, and I didn't realize that I knew so little about German war spies. I just wrote my story and thought it was wonderful. I persuaded Betsy, Ginny's older sister, who was now a junior in high school, to type it for me, and sent it away to a magazine very confident that it would be published and I would be famous.

After about three days, Ginny asked me at school one day, "Heard from your story yet, Ginny?"

"Not yet," I answered, "But I expect to any day."

"Oh, my, I'm going to have a famous story writer friend," giggled Ginny as she gave me a quick hug.

Day after day I waited to hear, each one of them seemed like a week, and finally six weeks had gone by. I was so sure now that they were going to publish it that I had even given up praying each night as I had been doing about it. I began to plan ways that I would spend all that money that they would send me.

It was a Saturday in late fall when Janice came dashing in from the mailbox waving a long white envelope and shouting, "You got your letter from New York, Ginny." One good thing about the goat being gone was that it had made Janice a happier person. She no longer screamed and cried all the time, but laughed and tried to do things to please people.

I had been drying the dinner dishes, which we always had at noon except in the wintertime, but on hearing her yell, I threw down the dishrag and ran outside to meet her. She handed me the envelope and sure enough it was from the magazine in New York, and it was addressed to Miss Ginny Haines. I was so excited that I could hardly tear open the flap. But what was inside was my story and a small piece of white paper. The paper fluttered to the ground while I stared at my story in amazement—surely they couldn't be returning my story after all that time! Janice handed me the paper and I saw the words staring up at me: "Sorry. It does not meet our needs." That was all. That was it. My first rejection slip.

All that afternoon I was crushed, but before supper I had hidden the rejection slip away with my story in a bureau drawer, washed my face and hands and found I was very hungry. I would write another story, or perhaps a play, and I knew they would sell.

I still had my dream and desire to be a teacher, and Mrs. Stillmore inspired me that it could be possible for after all, she was a teacher and she was a woman. Of all my older sisters, cousins, and the young women that I knew, no girl in our community of Hickory Grove had ever gone to college, and many of them hadn't even finished high school. And Naomi hadn't got to go at all. Well, I would be the first, I determined and I would become famous that way if I couldn't be a writer.

Mrs. Stillmore didn't let us older girls listen to the little ones' lessons as much as our men teachers had. She seemed to be more organized and knew just what she wanted to do. I supposed that she had had more college than they had, so knew more what to do. Sometimes, however, she got swamped, or a lesson with the older students ran over, and she asked me to "teach" the little ones. I was glad that Georgie Porgie was gone for I wasn't sure that I could endure sitting so close to him to listen to him read. The other Ginny knew that I enjoyed teaching more than she did so she usually let me have the job.

One beautiful autumn afternoon when we'd been explaining our annual wiener roast to the teacher and our time had run out, she asked me to stay in at afternoon recess to correct some math papers. I was sitting at the back of the room marking them with her red leaded pencil while she worked at her desk.

Suddenly she interrupted the silence by saying, "Ginny, have you ever thought about being a teacher?"

"Oh, yes, Mrs. Stillmore, I have for a long time, and I really want to be one." I stopped grading and looked at her with my best smile.

"Why, Ginny, why do you want to be a teacher?"

"I think it would be fun to teach kids, and I love to read, and I want to travel so I could share that with them, and also so the Milly Jeans of the world won't be catered to." I felt safe in saying that to her for she didn't cater to Milly Jean either which left that little one in a snoot most of the time.

At that, she laughed—a beautiful tinkling laugh. "I think that was one of my reasons to want to teach when I was a child too, but mine was Susan Jane."

I laughed with her and we went on grading papers.

"I have a dream about going to college and becoming a teacher," I said, but then added quickly, "But my family doesn't have any money to help me and I suppose it will cost a whole lot of money."

"Not as much as you might think," she answered. "There's a teachers' college in the southern part of the state and the tuition there is only seventy-five dollars for a whole year. And that includes books, activity fee, and health insurance. You have five years to save for it, and seventy-five dollars isn't that much."

When she said, "five years," I knew that I wasn't going to get to go on to high school with Ginny next fall, but I never gave up hoping. And when she said, "seventy-five dollars," I thought that may not be a lot of money to you, but to me, it might as well be a million. But at least I did have some hope that maybe I could achieve my dream someday.

That afternoon I took the little girls back to the woods to go hickory nut hunting. The trees were beautiful with their bright hues of gold, red, and orange. It was a time of year that I loved. Alice particularly loved doing this and many times begged me to take her hickory nut hunting even when there were no nuts to hunt. But this day we were in luck and soon had a big sackful to carry back to the corn crib where we spread them out to dry. Later we would take them to the house and on a cold evening when Mom was going to make cookies the next day, we would sit behind the heating stove and crack the hickory nuts with a hammer while we held them carefully on a brick. Then we would pick out the nutmeats for the cookies. We liked for Daddy to help for he could pick out two whole half nutmeats. Knowing how good the cookies would be, we could hardly wait!

We had a fine Christmas program and the teacher gave good treats, almost as good as Mr. Birkey had given us though she had just chocolate covered peanuts instead of the clusters, but I loved them too.

It was so cold that year that we had to stay inside most of vacation time. We couldn't even enjoy skating on the pond or playing in the snow. I started to write a new story about a little girl who lived in a little hut in the mountains with her grandfather, and it snowed so much they had to stay in all winter. I thought I knew a lot about this one for Mrs. Stillmore had just read us Heidi which was similar to my story. I would write during the day then make Janice and Alice help me act it out in the evening. They usually objected because I wanted them to be the goats.

Then before we knew it, it was March and time for our spring revival at church before the farmers would begin their spring planting. I had attended church and Sunday School since I was knee high to a duck, one of Daddy's favorite sayings, but I had not become a Christian, joined the church, and been baptized. But neither had Martha, or Ellen, or the other Ginny so I felt that since they were older than me that I was safe since they hadn't done this yet either. But on the first night of the revival that year all three of them went to the altar at the invitation to ask forgiveness for their sins and join the church. They were going to be baptized at the big church in Carmon the next Sunday afternoon as it was still too cold to baptize in the river as they did in the summertime.

This caused me to really think about my own condition and my need to make a decision for God. I knew that I had not done anything really bad like killing, or stealing — but then came the memory of when Ellen and I had stolen the watermelon from Old Mervin's patch, and I knew that God knew about that even if Old Mervin had never found out. The commandment about coveting also had me worried because I knew that I was always wanting things that other people had such as nicer clothes, bigger better houses, and delicious food in great abundance. The one about false witness I didn't quite understand so that night when Mom was up writing letters to my older sisters and brother who were away from home, I slipped out of bed and went into the living room where she sat in her old rocker close to the Aladdin lamp on the library table so she could see. When I touched her shoulder, she looked up in surprise.

"What are you doing out of bed, Ginny? Are you sick?" she asked — always the mother, always loving and caring.

"No, I'm not sick, Mom," I answered, "But I'm worried."

She laid her pen and paper on the table and pulled me down on her lap running her hand through my dark unruly hair. The long curls were gone, but it still lay in thick heavy waves on my head. Her kind brown eyes looked down into my green ones as though she were capable of solving all of the problems of the world as indeed I believed that she could.

"Now, Ginny, what is wrong?" she asked.

"I need to know what 'bear false witness' means," I said. "I'm not sure that I understand it, and I don't know if I have done it or not."

She smiled, but she did not laugh at my childish inquiry. Even though I was twelve years old, I was still a child to her. "Are you talking about the commandment in the Bible?" she asked.

"Yes, you know it says, 'Thou shalt not bear false witness. What does it mean?"

"Well, I suppose it means tell lies about people to hurt them," she answered. "Have you done that?"

I had been thinking about how cruel Ginny and I and the others at school had been to the Gralley children last year, but we hadn't told any lies for they had been dirty and smelly and they probably deserved to be treated the way we had, but somehow I didn't feel just right about that no matter what. But I decided that I wouldn't tell my mother about that just yet.

So, I answered, "No, I don't think so. I usually try to tell the truth. But what about that other one, the ad— Oh, you know, the a-d-u-l-t-e-r-y one," and I spelled out the word that I didn't know how to pronounce or what it meant. "What does that mean?"

I didn't know what I was asking my mother, who had let Martha tell me about babies in mommies' tummies, and periods and all sorts of things, something that she just couldn't bring herself to talk about. I didn't know, but neither did she tell me.

She sat for a long time in silence then she said, "That's a sin that grownups sometimes do, but you don't need to worry about it now, or even know about it now, Ginny."

"Oh," was all I said, but I wondered a lot about it.

Then my wise mother asked, "Are you thinking about becoming a Christian, Ginny?"

"Yes," I answered. "Yes, I am. Now that Martha and Ellen and even Ginny have, I'm really thinking about it."

"Well, instead of worrying about the Ten Commandments which no one can ever keep completely, you need to realize that the Bible teaches that everyone in the whole world has sinned and you can get forgiveness by asking God to forgive you and becoming His child. It's that simple, Ginny. Now, go to bed, or you'll never get up for school in the morning."

I kissed her goodnight and went back to bed to lie awake thinking about what she had said.

Next day at school while Ginny and I were eating our lunches in the swings, she said to me, "Don't you want to go to Heaven when you die, Ginny?"

And I answered, "Goodness yes, but I don't plan to die for a long, long time."

"But you never know when you might get real sick, or lightning might strike you," she said. "You better ask God to forgive you of your sins."

I thought about what she said all afternoon, but that night when we went to the revival meeting again, I didn't do anything about it. Thursday and Friday were just as bad, but on Friday night when the evangelist, who was much younger and certainly a better preacher than our old pastor, gave the invitation, I knew that this was the time for me, and I went to the altar to ask God to forgive me and to accept me as His child. I felt peace and happiness that I could now go to Heaven, but I still didn't want to die right away.

On Sunday afternoon, Vivian and Clifford, who had started attending church all the time now, took Martha and me to the church in Carmon to be baptized. Daddy went along, but Mom stayed home with the little ones though I knew she would have liked to have gone too. Mrs. Stillmore, who lived in Carmon, was a member of that church, and Ginny and I were very pleased that she came to our special service.

GINNY'S DREAM

Since I had only been to baptizing services at the river, I was amazed to find that this church had like a big bathtub at the front of the sanctuary where we were dipped down into the water while the minister prayed over us. We all wore white dresses and it was a special occasion in our lives. I felt good inside and when I said my prayers that night, I promised God that I'd try to be a better person from then on.

But I soon found out that even though you have given your life to God, your prayers are not always answered, at least not in the way that you want them to be. I had wanted a bicycle for a long time, and I had often prayed for one. Now, I felt certain that God would surely hear and answer that prayer.

Rex had a new one that one of his older sisters had given him, and wonder of wonders, he let me ride it. I had learned how on an old one that Ellen's dad had got for some work he did on someone's truck and had fixed up for them to ride. Ellen and Victor and even Milly, their mother, had spent long hours holding me up, running with me to get me started, then turning me loose to go on my own for a few wobbly feet before bike and me both crashed to the ground. Then they would pick me up, wipe off the dirt, or the tears, whichever the case—even sometimes having to take me inside to wash and bandage a cut—put me back on, and start all over again. Eventually, I learned and what a joyful day it was for all of us!

Then whenever they came up, or I went down to their house, (north was always up to us and south was always down), I would spend most of my time riding that old bike up and down the road, but never down their hill for that seemed a bit too scary.

Then about two weeks after the revival, I went home with Ginny to stay all night and there by the front porch stood Rex's shiny red bike that he'd gotten for his birthday. I wanted so badly to ride it, but was too scared to ask. I helped Ginny do her chores and then after supper dried the dishes, but still said nothing about wanting to ride the bicycle. We went out on the front steps where Betsy and Alma were doing their homework, and the bicycle was gone. Then I saw Rex coming up the lane peddling as hard as he could, his face flushed and hot. He rode up before the steps with a flourish and skidded to a stop.

"Want to try it, Ginny?" he asked and I knew that he was talking to me.

But before I could answer, Alma said quickly, "You better not, Rex. Remember Evelyn said not to let anyone else ride it," and my heart sank.

"It's my bike," Rex argued.

"But she gave it to you," Alma reminded him.

"Well, she'll never know. And Victor said that you could ride real good, Ginny, so come and give it a try." He got off the bike and brought it over to me.

I looked at Ginny for guidance and she nodded her head so I gripped those new shiny handlebars, flipped my leg over the seat and peddled across the yard and out to the lane. Before I was out of sight, I could hear Alma calling, "Just go to the end of the lane. Don't go out on the gravel road."

I didn't that day, but in the many days that spring and summer that I came back just to ride that bicycle, much to Ginny's dismay, I often ventured out on the gravel road and once I slipped on the loose gravel and fell over spraining my ankle so badly that it was swollen double by the time I limped painfully back to the house pushing the bicycle.

How I loved those rides racing along with the wind in my hair and pretending all the time that it was mine! I had wanted one for a very long time and used to pray at Christmastime that I would get a bicycle. This year I decided that maybe Elizabeth and Maurice would buy me one for my birthday, for I figured that they must have lots of money since he was a teacher and she worked at the dime store, and I knew that Elizabeth had always wanted one when she was growing up. I began to pray every night that this might be true.

One day in early summer when I had gone down to Ellen's, Rex was there on his bicycle. I asked him if I could ride it up to my house so I could show it to Mom. I wanted her to see what kind I wanted. He readily gave his consent and I was off. Still afraid of riding down their hill, I pushed the bicycle down and then got on down by the mailboxes. I was so happy that I sang to myself, "You Are My Sunshine" while I peddled up the road to our house.

Mom and my little sisters came out to see it, but she told me as she had so often in the past that they simply could not afford to buy me one. Janice wanted to ride it, and cried when I told her she couldn't. Then saying that I had to take it back to Rex, I took off, but at the little corner I turned north toward the creek instead of south toward Ellen's.

"Just one quick ride up this road," I told myself as I flew along. So caught up in my dreams of it really being mine that I forgot all about the steep hill at Jones's Bluff, I went down it so fast that it felt like I was flying. I became confused and forgot how to put on the brakes. I hit the bridge floor with a thud, and the next moment my heart came up in my throat, and I felt the worst kind of fear for the front wheel of the bike flew completely off and rolled to the side of the road while the rest of the bicycle and me ended up on the other side.

"Now, Evelyn will know for certain about me riding Rex's bike and she'll never let me do it again," was my first thought, and then not knowing what else to do, I sat down on the bridge and began to cry.

I don't know how long I had sat there when I heard a wagon coming and looking up, I saw Old Mervin coming towards me. On seeing me and the broken bicycle, he yelled "Whoa" to his horses, and said to me, "Are you all right?"

I wiped my eyes and my nose on the skirt of my dress and looked up. "Yes, but I've broken Rex's bicycle," and I began to cry again.

Before I realized what he was doing, he jumped down from the wagon seat, picked up the wheel and carried it over to where I sat. "Well, looks like it can be fixed.

Come along and I'll take you home. You're one of Joe Haines's younguns, ain't you?"

Yes, I'm the one who stole your watermelon, I said silently, but aloud I said, "Yes. But I need to get this back to Haases for that is where Rex is."

"Oh, well, Ethan can fix it for sure," he said and without more ado, he lifted the wheel and then the bicycle into the wagon and then gave me a hand to help me up. I hoped that Mom would not see us go by for I wasn't sure yet if I would tell her about what I had done.

Ellen's dad was able to fix it, Rex was not angry at me, and whether or not he told Evelyn, I didn't know, but he continued to let me ride his bike whenever I wanted. I thanked God for all of that, but I continued to pray for one of my own.

But I had made three important decisions this past year: I had decided that I would become both a teacher and a writer, I would go to college to prepare myself for those careers, and I had asked God to forgive my sins, and had become a Christian. I was happy about all three even though I couldn't understand why I couldn't get my prayers answered about the bicycle for I never did get one.

Chapter 15

Graduation

I was sad when school started that fall for Ginny had gone on to high school, and I was left alone. It also seemed silly to have to do seventh grade after I'd already had eighth. But that was the way it had to be so I tried to make the most of it. I soon became good friends with Nancy Austin who was now in sixth grade, and the year didn't turn out so bad.

I was now in the class with Rex, who I had left behind long ago, and a new boy named Jim McManus, who had recently moved in a new house down by the church. His dad was a supervisor or something in the oil fields that had come to great prominence to our community so we figured that he must be rich. Several new houses had been built for the workers and gas flares lit up the night sky on those farms fortunate enough to have had oil drilled on them. Now, it became the hope and dream of all of us to have oil drilled on our land so we could become rich too.

"I know what I'd get first thing," said my mom. "And that would be a bathroom. Wouldn't that be wonderful?" And it seemed like that was the consensus of most of the women in our community.

One of my dreams was that we could get the electric lines run from the schoolhouse to our house and have electricity. I thought that would be heavenly. I still hadn't been able to get together enough money to buy Mom a gas refrigerator like Mrs. Lawrence's, and with my plans to save money to go to college, it didn't look like I ever would. Oh, if only they would drill oil on our farm!

One good thing about school was that Mr. Grafton, the fun teacher who stood on his head on his desk and sang "Rattlesnakes Have Legs" was back as our teacher that year. We knew it would be a good year and we would do a lot with ball games and track. I didn't know then that I would become a player on the boys' basketball team for, of course, we started off with softball as that always came first. I was still playing first base, and I had become quite good at it. We all played without gloves so I wasn't made to feel poor because I didn't have one. But that year little Milly Jean decided to play, and wouldn't you know that she came to school the very next day with a new store boughten glove?

Everything was so easy to me because I'd already had eighth grade so I got to spend a lot of time that year teaching the little ones. Janice and Victor were in third grade, and I even got to teach them which I greatly enjoyed.

They needed someone to teach the little ones in Sunday School at our church so I volunteered for that too even though I was now old enough to join the young people's class, where Randall taught in the little room off the sanctuary, that I had so looked forward to being a part of. So, all that year I taught the little ones down in that dark basement at church, (the only good thing about it was that it was cool in the summer and warm in the winter since we had a real furnace down there), and I very much enjoyed doing the Bible stories for them, teaching them of God's love. I more than ever wanted to be a teacher.

I did get to be with the young people too for Randall started a youth group and we met every Sunday night at the church whether we had morning church or not. We had Bible study, games, and refreshments, and sometimes we had special parties. It was fun and I was happy to be back with Martha and Ellen and Ginny who had gone on and left me behind.

Almost every Friday afternoon we had a softball game with another school with them coming to our school, or us going to theirs. Since all of us older girls played on the team, there was no one to leave the little ones with so Mr. Grafton had to get some parents or someone to help take us to the games. The one who most often came was Aunt Lucy's granddaughter who was older than Martha and Ellen, but who had not gone on to high school. I couldn't understand why anyone would choose not to go to high school for I was certain that they had enough money as her dad had a big farm and this new Ford that Onessa so proudly drove. And if that wasn't enough, her grandma could have sold that car that set in her garage that I so longed for when I went there to stay the night with Martha. How I wished we had a car now that more and more people had them! When I grew up, I would have a beautiful new car and I would never ask anyone for a ride anywhere!

But Onessa came most every time to drive us to the other school, and we girls crowded into her car for the boys always rode with the teacher. I wondered if she would have let the Gralley girls ride in her car if they were still there. I wanted to ask her, but I didn't. She was a cheerful happy person who laughed and joked with us, and she always wore bright red lipstick. She wore it at home too which really surprised me for the other people I knew only wore makeup when they were going somewhere special. I always wanted to ask her why she hadn't gone on to high school, but I never had the courage to do so. But her younger brother David, who was in fifth grade, didn't go to high school when he graduated either. I decided that there was just no way to figure out some people.

When the weather got bad, we still got off every Friday afternoon for we had either a spelling bee, a geography match, or a ciphering match. I was good in spelling and geography, but not so good in arithmetic so I always hoped for the others.

For the spelling bee, we all stood across the front of the schoolroom in order from first grade up to us in seventh as there was no eighth that year. Then the teacher would sit in front of us with all the spellers in front of him, giving out the words to each child in turn. If after two tries a child missed a word, he or she had to sit down. The last person standing, no matter what grade they were in, was declared the winner.

For the ciphering match, we were divided into two groups: first through fourth and fifth through eighth, and we went to the blackboards which were on the west wall between the windows. There were also blackboards all across the back wall except where the furnace and the door were, but we used the west one so everyone could see. The teacher sent us two at a time and gave us a problem. The winner got to stay up until someone else beat them. There were always two winners, one for each group, and surprisedly enough it wasn't always the older ones that won. Victor was very good in math and usually came out a winner.

The geography match was just for the bigger kids. When we did it, the little ones got to play games like Going to the Mill and Fill in the Blanks on the back boards, draw and color pictures at their seats, or play with the big tray of little pictures that were on rubber pads so you could press them on the ink pad and then make little pictures on your paper. The school always furnished our paper and pencils so you didn't need to worry about wasting your own. They were always quiet so the teacher or us bigger kids didn't worry about them very much. For the geography match, the teacher would pull down a big map of the United States, or sometimes he would use

Europe or Africa. Then the person who was "It" would go to the board and find a place on the map, usually trying to not let us know where they were looking, unless you were a nitty like Milly Jean who would put her finger on it. Next they would print the first and last letter of the place and a blank for each missing letter. The person who found it first and spelled it correctly got to be "It" next. I loved playing this game, was good in it, and many times won.

We had always done this, but Mrs. Stillmore had made it more challenging last year because she gave prizes to the winners. As the oldest girl, I had decided to explain this to Mr. Grafton before we started doing them this year.

We now had a back door that led out to the basketball court that the directors had put in for fire safety. Nancy and I usually sat on the back steps to eat our lunch when we ate outside because she got a queasy stomach if she ate and swang at the same time. So, it was through the back door that I approached Mr. Grafton who was eating his lunch at his desk on the day that Nancy and I decided that someone needed to talk to him about the prizes. I walked to his desk and stood hesitant before him. He looked up with a smile.

"Well, Ginny?" he asked. "What's on your mind?"

"Mr. Grafton, you know about the spelling bees, geography and ciphering matches that we do in the winter time," I began.

"Yes, what about them?" he asked.

"Well," I wanted to tell him, but I felt kind of bad about it because it was like asking him to give us prizes which I guess was what I was really doing. "Well, you see last year Mrs. Stillmore gave us . . ." I really didn't see how I was going to do this after all.

"What did she do, Ginny?" he asked in a kind voice. "Surely Mrs. Stillmore didn't stand on her head on the desk and sing 'Rattlesnakes Have Legs,'" and I knew that he was teasing.

"No, of course not," I laughed. "She gave us prizes for being the winner. That way everyone worked very hard to be the winner and we all learned a lot. We just thought, that is Nancy and I did . . . "

"That maybe I would give prizes too?"

"Well, yes, but it doesn't have to be much. She just gave some candy or a new pencil or ruler or whatever. It wasn't much, but it was a prize."

"I think that's a good idea, Ginny, and I'm willing to do it. You can tell the others."

"Thanks," I said and went to the back door where Nancy was waiting and listening.

"Well, that was easy," she laughed shaking her blonde head while her blue eyes flashed. "He bought it so easily that you should have made the prizes bigger and better though."

"Nancy!" I whispered as I nudged her on down the steps. "That wouldn't be honest."

"Oh, Ginny," she sighed, "You're such a goody two shoes since you became a Christian."

I shrugged it off with a laugh, but I wondered if I had changed that much since I'd turned my heart over to God.

GINNY'S DREAM

We had our bees and matches all winter and I won several times, once even beating Victor out in the ciphering match on long division.

When the weather was bad, we also ate lunch inside usually sitting on the floor, or on the raised floor by the back blackboards, or at our desks. Then we had our marble tournaments where we drew lines with chalk on the oiled floor on each side of the room and then playing individually or by teams we shot at marbles all over the room. If you hit someone, they were dead, and if you killed everyone, you were the winner. There were no prizes for this, but a deep satisfaction if you won. My little sister Janice was very good, and if you escaped her deadly taw, you might, just might make it to the semi-finals.

It was an extremely bitter cold winter so we spent a lot of time indoors. We were all happy when Mr. Grafton brought a new game to school and taught us to play it. He brought it in from his car while we were all eating our lunches scattered about the room. We looked up when he walked in carrying a huge square board.

"What's you got there?" Rex asked from where he and Jim were eating at their desks.

"Come and see," invited Mr. Grafton. At his words, we left our lunches and ran over to the cover for the stairs that went down to the cellar where the furnace was. He set the board down and we noticed that it had little net pockets at each corner and there were lines across the board. Then he dumped out of a little bag some round wooden rings with holes in the middle of them, most of them were red or green, four were tan, and one was black.

They clattered to the board with a thud and we stared in amazement.

"What in the world is it?" asked Milly Jean, the first to get her tongue. "What kind of game is that?" If she didn't have one it probably didn't amount to a hill of beans anyway was what she was thinking.

The teacher laughed, but instead of answering, he moved the tan ones off the board, put the black one in the center and scattered the red and green rings around it. Then he picked up a tan ring and spun it on his finger.

"It's a game called carom," he said, "And the object of the game is to shoot those rings into these pockets," indicating the nets at each corner. You can play one against one, or as a team two against two."

"But how do you shoot them?" asked Jim McManus, who we supposed had been everywhere and seen everything.

"With this by using your finger," Mr. Grafton replied laying the tan ring down, doubling up his longest finger and letting it fly. Those rings scattered like everything and one red one landed in a pocket. "It's like pool for if your tan one goes in, one of yours comes out and you keep playing until you miss or go in the pocket. You have to stay behind these lines between each pocket and you can't move around the board so it's easier to have a partner. Any of you ever seen anyone play pool?" he asked.

We looked first at each other and then at him amazement on our faces for the only pool tables we knew anything about were in the taverns in Carmon, and we'd only heard of them for no children went in there, and no church members did either. So, we were surprised when Victor spoke up.

"Sure, I seen them," and before we could exclaim in surprise, he added, "I've gone in there with my dad and watched him play pool. This looks like fun."

It did look like fun and I wondered if it would be sinful to play it, but then decided quickly that since we weren't going to play it in the tavern, it probably wasn't.

"What's the black ring for?" I asked.

"That's the lucky one for if you knock it in, you get twenty extra points, the red and greens count one point each. The player or team that gets all theirs in first, gets all their opponents's rings left on the board."

Everyone wanted to try first and I thought for awhile there was going to be a knockdown fight, but the teacher, as usual, settled it by having us draw slips of paper with numbers on them. I was one of the lucky ones and got to play first. I was hooked from the very beginning for I loved that game. We raced now for the carom board instead of the swings every recess. But pretty soon the newness wore off and sometimes it was hard to find someone to play with. If no one else would play, I just practiced until the soreness in my fingers went away and I got really good. I could beat anyone even the teacher who sometimes challenged me.

Before it got so cold back before Christmas, the teacher began to practice with the basketball team on the outdoor court behind the building. It soon became evident to him that he didn't have enough big boys to make up a good team, and this sport minded teacher would have rather died than not been able to participate in the county tournament in Carmon in March. So, right away he asked Nancy and me if we would consider playing. He had seen us both fooling around on the court both before and after school and knew that we could dribble and shoot pretty well. We talked it over between ourselves, asked our mothers, and then told him that we'd be glad to play. So, we practiced with them until the weather got so cold that our fingers nearly froze for you couldn't play basketball very well with gloves on.

By the end of February, it had warmed up enough that we could begin to practice at recesses and after school, but was still pretty nippy in the mornings so no one stayed out except for Victor who lived and breathed basketball, and who practiced by himself if no one else was willing.

March was unusually mild and it seemed to me that we spent half the day practicing basketball. I had trouble getting all my work done and teaching the little ones too. I often had to take work home which was something that I hadn't been doing that year. But the tournament was coming up at the end of the month and he wanted us to be at our very best. Then he suggested something to Nancy and me that we both soundly rejected. He asked us to stay after practice one night the week before our first game.

"You girls are doing really well," he began, "And we all appreciate your helping us out in this way."

Nancy and I just smiled at each other for we loved playing and considered it our privilege to be able to. We wondered if he was going to throw us off the team, but knew he couldn't do that, or he wouldn't have enough players.

"You know that the boys wear uniforms for the tournament — shorts and jerseys."

We nodded our heads while both of us resolved that NO WAY were we wearing those things.

"I know that those aren't suitable for girls to wear, but I thought that if you wore shorts instead of slacks that you'd be freer to run and move about the court. What do you think?"

We thought for awhile then I said, "I don't know. I'll have to ask my mother first."

"Yes, so will I," Nancy agreed quickly. "We'll let you know."

But as we went around the building and out the front gate, we both knew the answer for this was 1945 and "nice" girls didn't wear shorts, particularly out in public places.

"I don't really want to anyway," Nancy volunteered after our looks at each other had verified what we were both thinking, and I smiled to myself for we'd just had another revival at church and this time Nancy had made her decision for God. Now, who was a goody two shoes?

We didn't wear shorts even though he actually begged us to, but we did play in the tournament, the only girls on any team, in the huge gym in Carmon. It was scary and mighty different playing ball on that floor under the bright lights instead of on our dirt packed court at Hickory Grove, but after we got the hang of it we really went to town. To the amazement of all, we won the tournament getting the big trophy and all the honors that went with it, and Victor was declared an honor player!

I still had my dream of going to college and becoming a teacher and an author. But now instead of just dreaming, I often talked about it at home, at school, at church, and at play. My mother would smile her sweet smile, wanting it for me, but knowing that it was probably impossible. Naomi was like Mom, but Elizabeth encouraged me for she had the same kind of dream even though she was married and already had a baby.

"Never give up on your dreams,"Ginny," she'd say while she nursed her baby and talked to me at the same time.

Martha and Ellen thought I was a dreamer, and sometimes even called me, "Joseph" in jest. Even Ginny who usually went along with all my plans, seemed to feel differently now that she was in high school.

"I'm going to take typing and shorthand courses," she told me, "And as soon as I'm out of high school, I can get a good paying job. Better forget about college, sweetie."

I didn't get much more encouragement at church either for all of them were hard working farmers who never thought of anything else. I often talked to Vivian, who'd gone all the way though high school back before I was born, and then married a farmer and that was it. But she could play the piano, and I felt that was a bit of refinement.

GINNY'S DREAM

"Just find you a good farmer to marry, Ginny, and your life will be happy," she'd say.

And at school they just laughed at me especially Milly Jean, who knew it took money to go to college and knew that I didn't have any. But I kept on dreaming.

We had two tragedies hit our community that spring. The first was that a little six year old girl, who lived in one of the new oil houses down by the church, suddenly became very ill and died. We were all shocked when we learned that she had polio, a terrible crippling disease. We'd heard them talk on the radio about President Roosevelt having this disease, and had read in the newspapers about people far away having it, but had never dreamed that it would come to our tiny community. It was a frightening experience for a child to die for it made us all feel more vulnerable. I prayed every night for a long time that I would never get polio. She and her little brother and sister had been coming to our Sunday School so had been in the class I taught. I wondered what it would be like to see a dead child, but they took her back to Pennsylvania where they used to live for her funeral and burial so we never saw her again. We always looked at their house whenever we passed it on our way to church and thought about the awful sadness that must dwell there. The little ones didn't come to Sunday School much after that and the parents never came.

The other incident was tragic too, but the way it was told to our family was so funny that this was often all we could think about.

GINNY'S DREAM

The war was still raging on in Europe, Africa, and Asia way across the ocean. Naomi's husband was in northern Africa, and we prayed for his safety each night. Joey was serving as an instructor in the Air Force so had escaped going overseas. He and Julia were out in Colorado with their baby daughter who had been born during the winter. I had three nieces and was only thirteen years old.

Somehow our small community had escaped any deaths so we were all shocked when we heard that the husband of one of the local girls had been killed. She had been a Phillips girl who had lived down by Matthews, the place where we now picked up apples that had fallen on the ground. She was Naomi's age, but I remembered when they lived there, and how she was often at our house, and I remembered how her long brown stockings were always wrinkled down by her ankles. So, we all felt sorry for her. Then one afternoon in early spring old Bob Bates who lived in the little cabin west of us with his brother and wife, (he's the one who played the fiddle and she's the one who told me all the wild tales and kept her suitcase packed to go to her son-in-law's funeral), came over to our house and told us his version of the news.

Old Bob was supposedly very hard of hearing, but my daddy always said that he could hear what and when he wanted to. He and Daddy were sitting in the old wooden rockers in the front room, which now Martha was trying to get us all to call the living room since Mom had moved her bed out of there into the dining room, and I was helping Mom sprinkle down clothes on the dining room table so we could iron them the next day. They were talking about the weather and the crops, and we weren't paying very much attention when suddenly he said something that caused us to perk up our ears.

"Guess you heard that Walter was killed in the war?"

"Yes," Daddy answered, "I did and I'm very sorry for Marilyn and his family."

"Yes, it was too bad," Old Bob responded. "I heard them say he got a purple heart."

"Yes, he did. All those wounded or killed in action get one."

Then very solemn-like our old visitor said, "That's what was wrong with him. He had a purple heart."

Mom and I both burst out laughing and had to escape to the kitchen, but poor Daddy was left there with him, and he told us later that he had a hard time keeping a straight face. Whenever anyone said anything about Marilyn's husband being killed in the war, we couldn't help thinking about him having a purple heart.

Before we could believe it was possible it was time for school to be out and my last days at Hickory Grove had drawn to a close. As the custom was, four of the one room schools in the surrounding area had a joint graduation program at the Methodist church in Applesville which was kind of a central point. It was also the custom for the graduating class to put on the program by either singing, reciting poetry or readings, or sometimes even skits. Since I was the only graduate from Hickory Grove, I decided to recite "Our Hired Girl" by James Whitcomb Riley, and much to my delight was able to get through all of it without faltering. Maybe I'd be an actress after all. Mr. Stillmore, as County Superintendent of Schools, was there to give the speech and hand out the diplomas. Mrs. Stillmore had come along and I was delighted to see her.

"Don't give up your dreams of going to college, Ginny," she said to me as she squeezed my hand.

"No, Mrs. Stillmore, I won't," I promised, happy that she still believed in me.

With my diploma in my hand, I was now officially graduated, and now had the long summer to get through before I could go on to high school. I dreaded going for we would have to ride the seven miles on the school bus and I didn't know very many kids on it, and the high school seemed so big when I'd gone to visit one day with Martha. But I knew that to fulfill my dream I had to do it one hurdle at a time and I was determined.

The summer passed quickly. When school was first out, we were terribly busy putting out the garden and hoeing the weeds, then there was dewberry and blackberry picking, canning them and things from the garden, and always the task of weeds. I was in 4-H Club again with Ginny and me being the older girls. Then in July we had our first Vacation Bible School at church. Ross and Danny, Vivian's little boy, were four years old that summer so they got to go too. They were so cute and we all nearly died laughing at them singing "This Little Light of Mine, I'm Going to Let It Shine" at Commencement night. Vivian taught my class and we girls embroidered dresser scarves for our project. It had been fun and it helped the summer to pass.

Daddy's birthday was the 27th of June and we had started having our family reunion close to that date. Since the war in Europe was over, and it was hopeful that the war with Japan would soon be over, it was easier to request a certain time for a furlough so Joey and Julia were there that year too. Only Larry was still away. Daddy's birthday was on a Sunday so we planned the reunion for that day. He was fifty-eight years old on that birthday for he was much older than my mother who was only forty-three.

Naomi and her little girl and her in-laws came as well as Elizabeth, Maurice, and their little girl. Joey, Julia, and their baby had already been with us for a week so they got to help with the preparations. Vivian, Clifford, and Danny always came too as did Grandma, Aunt Marie and Uncle Leonard as well as Randall and Sarah. Ellen was always there when we had a family get together. So, it ended up quite a crowd.

We set up long tables made of boards and covered with tablecloths out under the maple trees. Everyone brought food and we cooked for days. With all the garden stuff, fresh berries, and frying chickens it was quite a feast.

Martha, Ellen, and I were sitting with our filled plates on our laps and our backs against a huge tree enjoying the food, when we heard Ross and Danny talking on the other side of the tree. What they said amused us so much that we nearly choked on our food.

"Is this meatloaf?" asked Danny as he speared a piece of meat on his fork.

"No," replied Ross in all of his four year old dead seriousness. "This is a reunion."

Then suddenly it was the middle of August, the week before my fourteenth birthday, and almost time for school to start. Daddy and I were down at the barn in the twilight of a summer evening getting ready to do the milking.

As we sat down on our stools and put the buckets under the cows' udders, he said to me, "Are you really serious about this college business, Ginny?"

"Yes, I am, Daddy, very, very serious."

Then he said something that would have surprised the socks off me if I had been wearing any. "Each year you are in high school I'll try to save a little money for you, and when you graduate I'll sell a calf or a pig and give you that money. So, count on going, Ginny, and don't ever give up that dream."

"Oh, Daddy," I got up off my stool and went to hug him while tears came in my eyes. "But won't the others be jealous if I get to go?"

"I don't think Martha's too interested, it's too late for the older ones, and we'll worry about the younger ones when they get there. You see, Ginny, once long before you were born I had another girl, my Alice from my first wife, who had a dream of being a nurse, and I sold a calf to send her to Chicago to become a nurse. But she never quite made it for she caught pneumonia and died. I want you to have the same chance that she had, and I know you'll make it."

There were tears in his eyes too as we hugged there in the entryway of that old barn while the cows looked at us in bewilderment, swishing their tails and mooing.

And I did, just like Daddy said I would. Just like I dared to dream.